Strange Affairs

Rotonger Burns

iUniverse, Inc.
New York Bloomington

Strange Affairs

iUniverse books may be ordered through booksellers or by contacting:

iUniverse
1663 Liberty Drive
Bloomington, IN 47403
www.iuniverse.com
1-800-Authors (1-800-288-4677)

ISBN: 978-1-4401-9205-0 (pbk)
ISBN: 978-1-4401-9206-7 (ebook)

Library of Congress Control Number: 2009912012

Printed in the United States of America

iUniverse rev. date: 11/19/2009

Chapter One

In early June, on another sunny, summer morning in Phoenix, Arizona, Johnny Lambert, crawled out of his bed at 7:00 am at his new luxurious two bedroom apartment on the south side of Phoenix, Arizona, just before he had to report to work at Lancaster Lane Building Corporation, where he was an executive manager and the company lawyer.

Lancaster Building Corporation was located on the first floor of a tall glass building in the south side of Phoenix, Arizona. Johnny had twenty office employees that were under his administration. His office secretary was Sallie Long Heart. He worked very closely with her. She kept his paper trail and appointments very organized. He valued her work ethics very much.

All of his employees respected him. He was very good at the dual role he was working at the corporation. The only thing that was missing, according to his family, was a woman that he could settle down with. Although Johnny was only twenty nine years old, he was very successful and his family was proud of his accomplishment. He was very driven in accomplishing his goals.

Johnny had been out late parting with one of the beautiful women that he picked out of his long list of names located in his treasured black book. Johnny was truly looking for love in all the wrong places. He had drifted far from the teachings that his parents had given to his younger brother, sister, and himself. To Johnny, they were the perfect example of how two soul mates were to express their love, but he struggled in finding the woman that he could love and be with for a lifetime.

As Johnny hurriedly picked out some clothes to wear, he said out loud, "I have to stop hanging out so late with different women, but, oh it feels so good." Johnny loved burning the candle at both ends. He worked hard in the daytime at his office, but at night he partied with beautiful women with the same driven purpose. Although Johnny would love to settle down as his family wanted him to do, he felt as if he was having too much fun being single.

Besides, Johnny felt that unless the woman that he would choose to marry had the same basic value system that his parents shared, he would not waste his time in committing to her. Johnny took out his black tailored suit, white shirt, grey tie and black Stacy Adam shoes. He laid them out on his lounge chair. He took a quick shower, got dressed, rushed down stairs and fried two pieces of bacon, toasted two pieces of wheat bread, and ate it on his way to work along with a bottle of orange juice that he got out of his refrigerator.

Johnny made it to work at 9:00am. As he was closing the door of his black 2009 Lexus, trimmed in Gold, 300 GS fully loaded vehicle, he saw a beautiful woman that had long thick black hair with a trim built that was approximately 5'6 inches tall. She had on a grey two piece business suit with a black belt and black pumps. He could not see her face, but it was something about her grace and the hop in her seductive walk that drew him to her. Johnny looked at his watch, and said, "I had better hurry and get to my desk before my employees look at me strangely because I am always stressing to them on how they need to be at work on time, and here it is, I am almost late." Johnny made it to his desk on time, but could not focus on his work because all he could think about was the mysterious woman he saw in the parking lot with the hop in her sexy walk that was so drawing to his inner being.

Sallie, Johnny's secretary, walked into his office and said, "Good morning, Mr. Lambert, Mr. Lincoln called you earlier to set an appointment with you to close the deal of the apartment complex that is to be built in the center area of Phoenix, Arizona." Johnny said, "Okay Sallie, please have him to stop by at his convenience. I will be here until 3:00 pm. I am leaving the office to take a late lunch, and I will return at 4:00pm. From that point on, I will be in the office from 4:00pm until 9:00pm." Sallie said, "Okay Sir. I'm calling him as we speak."

Sallie often took the office wireless phone every where she went so that she would not miss any calls because many of their clients complained about their automatic answering service. Johnny pulled it together just long enough to wrap up the paper work on the Penn Hotel deal in Orlando, Fl that is due to be built in six months , in late February. When 3:00 came, Johnny neatly stacked the finished paper work of the Penn Hotel deal in a black notebook that was labeled Penn Hotel and put it in his locked file cabinet for safe keeping. Johnny put a copy of the original file of the Penn Hotel plans in another designated file cabinet. He always kept an extra copy of his original paperwork so that he could have a backup source.

As Johnny walked out of his office, he stopped to talk to Sallie. "Sallie, I'm going across the street to the Easy Meal diner for lunch. Please, take any messages for me that come in and put them on my desk. I will return them when I get back." Sallie said, "Ok, Mr. Lambert." By the way, I talked to Mr. Lincoln, and he told me that he would try to come at 5:00 pm, if that is alright with you." Johnny said, "Yea, that is fine." Sallie called Mr. Lincoln back and confirmed the appointment. Sallie had been with the company for a total of eleven years. Johnny had only been with the company for six years. The both of them worked very well with each other.

She definitely had her skills down to a science, not to mention, her professionalism was unmatched. She was a beautiful petite thirty year old woman with sandy light brown hair, hazel eyes, high cheek bones, small nose, and small full lips. She made it known that she had a no nonsense attitude toward office romances. She was also very private about her personal life. He did not know anything about her family or if she had any living family members. Johnny did not know anything about Sallie outside of work.

However, it was something about Sallie that drew him to her. He often appreciated a woman with values that respected and carried herself in a lady like manner like his mother and younger sister. He never pressured Sallie to tell him about her family or life outside of work because he did not mention his family that often around her.

Although from time to time he made reference of his family very casually to her and some of his buddies that he played basketball and went on adventurous hiking trips with.

Johnny walked into Easy Meal diner, and sat at his usual corner table in the back of the diner. This area had dimmed lights, was very relaxing, and had a big window used to watch incoming and outgoing customers. He began to think about his experiences that he had with love. He realized that he has only experienced ordinary love but not extraordinary love. He wondered to himself was it more to love than what he had already experienced? He said to himself, "I have enjoyed good love making, but I don't know if I have experienced extraordinary love yet."

Linda his waiter and best friend came to his table and asked him as she greeted him with a warm smile and a hug, "What would you have today, Johnny?" Johnny said, "Hi, Linda, I would like a petty melt and fries with a diet Dr. Pepper." Linda was a young lady that Johnny had dated for several months, but the both of them agreed to stop dating because they acted more like sisters and brothers. Instead of acting like a couple they wrestled and played basketball and video games the majority of the time they were together. They still remained great friends that looked out for one another. This was the very reason why he ate lunch at the Easy Meal diner almost every day so that he could talk to Linda about his daily issues, if she was not too busy. In addition it was a hot spot for famous celebrities. Linda told Johnny, "Ok, I will bring this back, as soon as we are done." Johnny said, "Thank you, I will be here."

As Johnny waited, he looked out the window, and began to think about the lady he saw this morning with the grey suit and black pumps that walked so seductively and sexy that it almost blew his mind with excitement. As he began to think on her beauty and sex appeal, he suddenly saw her walking toward the diner. As she began to walk by the diner, he caught a glimpse of her face.

Until that moment, he did not really know how she looked from shoulder up. He only knew that she had a gorgeous small curvy body. It was very appealing. She was a true brick house. He could tell that she was the true picture of beauty. She had long, thick, shiny, black, straight hair with a touch of redness that glowed in the sunlight. She had beautiful slightly slanted black eyes, small straight nose, high cheek bones, and a perfect set of white teeth. Her lips were slightly round and plump. They were so inviting that it was hard for him to look at her without lusting.

Johnny had to finally turn his head because she was almost too much to bear even while looking at her from a distance. The mysterious woman had already crossed the street by the diner and was heading toward the next building along the same side of the road. Johnny, without hesitating, ran to the front door of the diner, as he watched her go into the next building. He said out loud shaking his head with despair, "Boy, I missed my chance to talk to the mysterious woman that has graced my mind with thoughts that I wouldn't even want to share with my closest buddies." Johnny wondered what nationality she was because he could not tell. You could not really pin point her from one race to the other. She just looked multi cultured. As far as he was concern, it did not matter to him what nationality the woman was that he was interested in, as long as he enjoyed her company.

As Johnny stayed there looking in amazement at the next building, he could not help, but too have a pit in his stomach because of the pain he felt when he could not reach her in time. Not soon after, he came to himself. He blinked when he noticed that she was coming out of the building shouting, "Taxi, Taxi, stop, please!" Johnny was again mesmerized by her beauty. He could barely concentrate. All he could do was focus on her little pouty lips that were just plump enough to be enticing, not to mention, the luscious red colored lipstick that made her look even more exotic and sexy.

He said out loud, "Wow, where have you been all of my life?" Of course, she did not hear him nor could she single him out in the large crowd of people. The mysterious woman stepped into the taxi, and rode away. To Johnny's dismay, he walked back into the diner, and sat back into the corner table in the back. Shortly after he had sat at his table, Linda was approaching his table with the lunch he had ordered.

Linda turned and faced Johnny and began to say, "Johnny, you sure were in a hurry. Where were you going? I thought you were going back to work without paying for the lunch you ordered. Is everything alright? Johnny, you know I would have been very angry with you for that. You know I work hard for my money. Besides all that, I expect a big tip before you leave this table." Johnny said to Linda, "Linda, you know I'm always looking for my next love quest. I keep seeing this mesmerizing woman that walks with a hop that has a sexy swagger to it. She is driving me crazy every time I think about her. She really turns me on. I really would love to get to know her." Linda said, "Ok, watch out, Johnny. Hold your horses. You know what happened the last time when a girl excited you that much. In fact, we both know what happened with that."

Johnny looked at her smiling with his dark black hair that was cut in a fade and big beautiful brown eyes with extremely long eyelashes that was almost too pretty to be on a man. Besides all of that, Johnny was at least 6 feet 4 inches tall on a lean muscular body that could beat any male model walking down a runway. In addition, he had the most enticing muscled chest that could easily be noticed in his finest expensive dress shirt. My, my, my, don't mention him in a short sleeve shirt and blue jeans.

He also had highly defined muscular legs and nicely shaped behind that was highly noticeable and amazing for any woman to see. Johnny was the picture of handsome that every woman noticed in any setting. She remembered this all too clearly the brief times they went out. Women would drool when they looked at him. His appearance was like looking at a great Greek god that came alive just to give women the pleasure of looking upon his masculinity.

Linda, came back to herself, and realized that even though they acted more like sisters and brothers, he still possessed very handsome qualities that women rarely came across.

Linda turned toward Johnny and sat down at the table with him and began to say, "Johnny, there you go. You already know that you are a good man. Not to mention that you have handsome qualities that you rarely see, but don't you think that it is about time for you to think about settling down with a good woman. Instead of just running behind a beautiful woman that excites you to a boiling point. Now don't get me wrong, everybody enjoys beauty. Heck, you grace us regularly with your handsome self, but the fact still remains. Isn't it time for you to be done with going from woman to woman, and settle down with one good one. Yea, I often hear about your late night creeping. Have you not grown tired of that, yet?"

Johnny turns to look at Linda, as he swallows some of the patty melt he had been devouring since she first gave it to him, and said very charismatically, "Linda, you know that I have been looking for love in all the wrong places. I'm really not looking to settle down at this time in my life. I just, really want to get my freak on, or have you forgotten all about that." Johnny loved picking on Linda and pushing all of her buttons.

Linda voices, sarcastically, "Now Johnny, it is a known fact that what we had together was good. Well, I must say, it was really good, but we acted more like brothers and sisters than anything else. We were always wrestling and playing around. Even when we were intimate those few times, it was so romantic and intense, and felt so, so, good, but the other part of our relationship felt kind of strange. We both talked about if we could live off the romantic portion of our relationship that would be beautiful. However, after the romance was over, we still had that brother and sister type thing going on that seemed a little weird. Now, have you forgotten that so soon, my dear?

She smiled as she filled his glass with more diet Dr. Pepper. The owners never bothered her when she was with Johnny. They loved her like a daughter, and wanted her to marry a nice guy like Johnny. Besides, they could see how amazingly close they were. Although the owners did not know that the two of them had already came to the conclusion that they would be nothing but friends.

Johnny said, 'Linda you know that I have not forgotten that. Although, I still miss those intimate moments. We had a hot and steamy romantic relationship." Linda looked at Johnny and rolled her eyes at him and said, "Will there be anything else?" Johnny said, "Linda, you know I am just joking with you. I know that even though the romantic side of our relationship was wonderful, the both of us knew that we acted more like sisters and brothers. This is what made our relationship as a couple very awkward. Linda, you know that I still love you and you will always be my girl." Linda said, "Yea, like a sister." Johnny replied, "Yes, like a sister, just to please her, but he often thought how great it would be to be married to his best friend. Johnny never pursued this thought because it was clear how Linda felt, and he would rather have her as a best friend versus not having her in his life at all.

After that, Linda walked away from the table to wait on other customers that had entered the diner. Johnny finished his lunch, and signaled to Linda, by raising his hand, for her to bring him his ticket. Linda noticed him. She brought his ticket to his table and laid it in his hand. Johnny reached into his pocket, and pulled out a twenty dollar bill. He told her to keep the change. He also left an extra ten dollars at the table for her tip. Linda was a very special person to him as well as his best friend. However, before he left, he asked Linda to spend just a few more minutes with him after she had waited on her last customers. They had discussed earlier that they had moved from their previous apartments to a new location and was suppose to give each other their new addresses.

Johnny knew that he was pressed for time. As he looked at his watch, he noticed he had only fifteen minutes to spare. He took a few moments to call Sallie at the office to let her know that he was going to be a little late coming back from lunch. He told her if Mr. Lincoln came a little earlier than expected, to entertain him by offering him something to drink or something from the deli that was across the hall. Sallie told him that she would handle everything until he got back. Linda had already told Johnny, that she would come back when she was finished handing her last customer his take out meal that he ordered.

As Linda approached Johnny's table, he looked very seriously at her, and began to question her about the beautiful woman he had saw in the parking lot this morning, and during lunch. Linda told him that she had not noticed her, but now that she knew that he was interested in her, she would keep her eyes and ears open. She told him that if she heard anything she would let him know. Due to Johnny having to get back to the office, he and Linda forgot to exchange their new addresses. Johnny rose from the table and kissed Linda on the cheek.

He walked outside of the diner to go back to work. It was beautiful in down town Phoenix. The business offices and shopping areas were very industrial and modern, but they also had a tropical flare to them with the implanted palm trees and beautiful cactus plants that surrounded all of the buildings. Not to mention the dryness to the sunny days that inspired the locals to dress casually in shorts and T-shirts when they were not at work. He hurried back to the office watching out for the busy traffic that was between the diner and his office.

He was excited about talking with Mr. Lincoln about the apartment complex project to be built in the center downtown area of Phoenix, Arizona. They were targeting middle class families or couples. As Johnny walked into the office, he was met by Sallie informing him that Mr. Lincoln would be arriving at 5:00 pm. Sallie asked Johnny if he needed her to run any copies or make any refreshments for his meeting.

Johnny said, "Yes, please. This is the original copy of the proposal. Can you make me two copies of it and make the refreshments that you know he would find delightful." Sallie replied, "Yes, I can handle that. I will be happy to do this for you. I will do anything to help everything flow properly." The two of them was so compatible in their working relationship. They have been working together for about six years.

Johnny often fantasized what they would be like as a romantic couple. If only she believed in office romances. Sallie felt that office romances always ended badly. Thusly, making the working relationship very difficult to handle after the romantic love affair was ended. Sallie had a no-nonsense attitude about this subject because she had seen it too many times in the past with other office employees. So, she vowed to herself, that she would never engage in such a relationship that would put the job she loved in such a predicament. Besides, she loved working with Johnny, and she often admired him for his handsome looks.

She personally wished that he would just settle down and stick to one good woman. He often told her of the heavy dating he did at the clubs, almost every night when he got off of work. Frankly, she did not know how he came to work on time and was so relaxed the next morning. Sallie had let Johnny know, early on, how she felt about office romances could do more harm than good in destroying a descent working relationship. Although he knew this, he still complimented her on how she looked and carried herself. He had asked her out multiple times, when he would see her in the grocery stores or in the street outside of the office, but she would not give in to his continued advances.

The two of them worked through those advances and were able to create a great working relationship. Besides, she knew that Johnny was a good man. It was something about how he reverenced her and respected her work. She would never think about pressing a sexual harassment charge on him. She felt like that would be too much. She knew that he did not mean her any harm. She felt like he was the kind of man that she would give a chance. If only he would settle down with one woman and he did not work with her.

At 5:00 pm, Mr. Lincoln showed up for his appointment with Johnny. As Mr. Lincoln entered the office, he noticed Sallie sitting at her desk. "Hi, Ms. Sallie, How are you today? It is so warm outside today. I love Phoenix, Arizona. That is why I talked my wife, Lola, into moving down here from North Carolina when we first got married." Sallie voiced, "Yes, it is very beautiful in Phoenix. I love it here also. I cannot deal with cold weather." Mr. Lincoln voiced, "Yes, it is beautiful here. It was so nice to see and talk to you Sallie. Is Mr. Lambert in?" Mr. Lincoln spoke very professionally with a strong masculine voice.

Mr. Lincoln was a middle aged man about fifty years old that was very handsome and tall. He was about 6 feet 3 inches. He had a muscular built. In addition, he had very deep greenish eyes, small nose, full plump lips, and beautiful wavy brown hair with a few grey strains that made him look very distinguished. He had a full head of hair with no sign of hair receding. Yes, indeed. Mr. Lincoln was a fine man. Sallie thought to herself, besides Johnny, men that handsome did not come along that often.

Mr. Lincoln was often approached by many women on a regular basis from the ages of 20-60 years old. Sallie liked the idea that Mr. Lincoln was very devoted to his wife of thirty years. He told Sallie one day that he did not have a reason to step out of his marriage because his wife satisfies all his need. He also said that his wife was the most beautiful woman that he has ever known. He loved that she had a pleasant, spiritual presence. Sallie said under her breath, "Yes, Yes, Yes, I would love to have a man similar to Mr. Lincoln, but he would definitely have to be a Christian."

Mr. Lincoln also told Sallie at an earlier time, that in his twenties, before his wife snatched him from that lifestyle, he was a high roller. He was known to be a womanizer. He often had two women that he was dating at one time. They were his wife and a woman on the side. He found out early on, in his early teens, how women went wild over him. His growth spurt happened when he was thirteen years of age and he was already growing a mustache that made him look even older.

His wife, Lola, finally gave him an ultimatum by telling him when she caught him with his other woman at a restaurant, "This is the last draw. Either let that other women go, or go outside this house and never come back." She told him that his clothes were already packed and placed in the street up above their house on a hill. So, he had better make up his mind, quickly, before his clothes were stolen when people found out how expensive they were.

Of course, Mr. Lincoln chose his wife. His wife also made it known that he also had to go with her to marriage counseling for a year under her Pastor, J.C. Burns. Yes, Lola was a Christian woman that believed in the sanctification of marriage. Mr. Lincoln agreed, and in the process of rebuilding their marriage and good old fashion Christian counseling, Mr. Lincoln renewed his Christian values and repented from his adultery. He was thankful and very satisfied with having only one good woman for the rest of his life.

Sallie thought that Mr. Lincoln could be a great witness to Johnny helping him to stop dating so many women at one time, and to settle down with one good woman. Sallie asked Mr. Lincoln to have a seat while she let Johnny know that he had made it. Johnny stood up, and went out to greet Mr. Lincoln. "Hi, Mr. Lincoln, How are you? You can come into my office. Sallie has prepared refreshments for us to enjoy during our meeting. Help yourself. She already told me that she knew the kind of snacks you liked. They are very good. I've already had some."

Mr. Lincoln replied, "Yes one day when you were out, I had stopped by, unannounced, to talk with you about the new developments of the apartment complexes. Sallie was already enjoying some of her favorite snacks and we began to talk about the snacks we had in common." Johnny said, "Oh yes, Sallie told me that I had just missed you when I came back from a late lunch. Sorry, about that." Mr. Lincoln said, "That is quite alright. We will talk about the new developments with the apartment complexes during this meeting." Johnny said, "That is good." So the two men discussed the plans for the development of the new apartment complexes in Phoenix, Arizona, as well as the new developments of the blueprints of the shape and square footage of each two to three bedroom units.

The two men concluded the meeting by setting the start date of the construction plans which was to be on November 1st of this year according to what the builders had previously discussed with Mr. Lincoln. The project of the apartment complexes would take at least eight months to get at least three to four buildings finished. The other remainder four buildings would be finished in the middle of the next coming year, totaling eight- four story building in a twelve month period.

Just as Mr. Lincoln was leaving out of Johnny's office, Johnny stopped him and gave him a copy of the plans to build the apartments and the proposal of the builders. Johnny asked Sallie to make some additional copies of the things that they discussed during this meeting so that he could place them with the other original documents and lock them up in his designated locked file. Sallie did so and also said her goodbyes as she left for the evening. Sallie had already asked Johnny to let her leave an hour early in order to make it to Wednesday night bible study that started at 7:00 pm. The office usually closed at 8:00 pm on Wednesday to help get things together before the upcoming Friday when they usually closed at 12:00 noon.

As Sallie was leaving, she said to Johnny, "Goodnight Sir. Have a good evening." Johnny replied, "You too Sallie. Don't forget to send up a prayer for me." Sallie said, "Oh, I never miss a day without praying for you. I pray for you all the time."

Johnny continued to look at the plans for the building of the apartment complexes in Phoenix, Arizona. He made a few more phone calls to the contractors, electricians, home interior decorators, and plumbers, so that the project would go as smoothly and on schedule as possible. Johnny also called his date to see if things were still on for tonight. Of course, his date confirmed that it was still on, who could resist a man like Johnny.

Chapter Two

After making all the calls to the various professionals involved in building the apartment complexes in down town Phoenix, Arizona, he left the office to go pick up his date. Her name was Mary Phelps. It was a very warm evening. The sun was setting and the earth tones of the building were so beautiful at the shadow of the sun set. Johnny arrived at Mary's house at 9:30 pm. As soon as he arrives, Mary greets him at the door, and says, "Come on Johnny. I am ready to party. I have been waiting on this all day."

Johnny replied, "Hi Mary. How are you?" Mary very hastily pulled him toward the car, as if she was about to burst. Johnny said, "Slow down, Mary. The movie does not start until 10:30 pm, and it is just down the street." He could already smell the faint smell of alcohol already on her breath. It quickly turned him off. It was alright in the beginning, but he was beginning to notice she had a problem with alcohol. He has only dated her about three times, but each time he picked her up, she smelled like alcohol.

They went to see, "Crazy Horse", the movie at the Twilight movie theater. When the movie was over, they went dancing. Mary was a tall cream colored, twenty five year old woman with long straight blonde hair. She put you in the mind of a Super model just waiting to be discovered. She had a graceful appeal about her that Johnny liked, at least until he found out she had a problem with alcohol that did not mind drinking as many drinks that was offered to her, even if it was four or more drinks in one setting.

Mary seemed to be having a great deal more fun than Johnny was while they were out together. She not only danced with Johnny, but also with every man that walked in her direction. Johnny could tell that she was getting more and more tipsy, but because she was so beautiful, he continued to tolerate her. Besides, he was looking for a little extra, once he dropped her off at home. It wasn't until Mary began to climb up a table and began to take off her clothes, when Johnny said to her, "That is enough, Mary. It is time that we get out of here." Mary replied, "No, the party is just getting started." Johnny angrily said, "Mary, either you come with me now or I am leaving you here!" He knew he had to get a little stern with her because she could be very persistence in her ways.

Mary decided to leave with Johnny without fighting with him. Although she was drunk, she knew she wanted to go out with Johnny again. She knew that he was one of the greatest eligible bachelors in the entire Arizona state. Johnny drove up to Mary's front door, and walked her to the door. He kissed her on the forehead and said, "Good night. I will call you later in the week." Although, Mary tried desperately to get Johnny to come in for a night cap, Johnny would not give in. He left, thinking to himself that tonight was the last straw. He would never ask her out again.

Johnny did not mind his dates drinking sociably, but he did not want them to show any signs or symptoms of being drunk. Johnny was attracted to strong independent women with integrity, strong values that knew what they wanted out of life, and worked hard to get it, in an honest way. Someone like Sallie, he thought honestly. Johnny wished that she would give him a chance to get to know her better. He was sure he could convince her to be in a relationship with him. If only she was not so hard to get. That very thing made him want her even more.

Chapter Three

As Johnny was driving home, he thought earnestly how he would pursue the woman that had the very sexy walk. He felt like he would not have a chance with Sallie as long as they worked together. He was not about to change their working conditions because he wanted to be around her in one way or another. Besides, he had his mind set on the woman with the sexy walk. He felt strongly that if he had a chance to talk with her, he would be able to make her his special lady. Johnny was still sowing his oats. He was not ready to be committed to one person, since he broke up with Linda. Despite how he agrees with Linda about their relationship being like sisters and brothers, he really felt that she was the most compatible woman he had ever dated. One that he really could see himself having a lasting relationship with.

He and Linda did not see the same things. No matter how he tried to agree with her, he really felt like they were the best romantic couple that he had ever experienced. Nevertheless, he would not dare share this information with her because he did not want to destroy their beautiful friendship. Again, he wanted to take what he could get, just to satisfy his need to have her and Sallie in his life. No matter how he wanted more from them. He made the sacrifice to keep them an everlasting part of his world, or at least as long as the ride took them.

Johnny was approaching his apartments, when he noticed a small red Toyota parked on the curb by his apartment. He wondered to himself whose vehicle it belonged to because he never seen it parked there before. He thought to himself, this looks like Sallie car, but he dismissed it because he felt like she would not be out anywhere so late at night.

He took a shower and went to bed. He got up at his usual time and ate his usual breakfast. He also made it to work at his usual time. As Johnny drove into the garage apartment, he hoped that he would see the woman with the sexy walk. Unfortunately, he did not, so he rushed into his office before he was late. As he walks by Sallie's desk, she greets him with a beautiful smile, and says to him, "Good morning, Sir. I hope you had a pleasant night." He replied, "Yes, it was very enjoyable." He wanted to tell her how it would have been even better if she would have accompanied him, but he did not want to start anything that Sallie might have became offended by.

They both worked hard that day to catch up on a lot of unfinished business concerning the apartment complexes in Phoenix, Arizona, and went home to their other lives outside of work. Again, Johnny picked up one of his dates and partied all night long, without a care in the word, with wild loose women. He often thought to himself, "Why do I choose the kind of women that I would not even take to meet my cousin, much more to meet my immediate family." He soon dismissed that thought with the rationale, that he was young, handsome, and having fun, not really knowing the trouble he was setting himself up for.

As he was driving home, again, he saw the small red Toyota parked at the curb. He went into his apartment and went fast asleep as soon as his head hit the pillow. As he slept he dreamed more and more about the woman that had the sexy walk, and that he would love to meet her. He thought about how he could try to approach her in order to get to know her better. He was confident that she would love to go out with him if only given the opportunity to talk with her.

In his dream, he was as smooth as Billie D. Williams and Brad Pitt put together. He was as charismatic as President Barack Obama speaking to crowds both small and great. Yes, Johnny was laying the charm mighty thick, and he was doing just what he sought out to do, and that was to make that woman his very own Queen of the Niles. Johnny was so engaged in this dream that he almost did not hear his alarm going off. He quickly showered and got dressed and drove as quickly as he could to work. He could not afford to waste any more time in making breakfast because he had already over slept. He used his alarm clock as a second resort to wake up, because he normally got up 20 minutes prior to it alarming. However because the dream was so good, and he was so smooth with the woman with the sexy walk, he over slept.

Chapter Four

As Johnny drove from home to the office, he looked out his window to see a young mother and father scrolling their little baby in the park. He wondered will he ever find a woman that he could fall in love with and spend the rest of his life with. He wanted to have a big family. He loved children so much. His mom and dad taught his younger brother, sister, and himself how to respect and love each other. He remembered how his mom and dad loved each other so much. He could only hope and pray that he would find that kind of love before it was too late.

Johnny drove into the company parking lot. He started to think about the young woman he had seen the other day that really sent his heart racing. He was hoping to see her again today, but thought that was to near to impossible. He got out of his car and walked into his office. A beautiful woman with a beautiful smile greeted him. He did not pay a great deal of attention to the woman other than noticing she had a beautiful smile. She was sitting at Sallie's desk with a cup of coffee in her hand ready to give it to him as he walked inside the office.

She said, "Hello, I'm Rosalyn. Sallie will not be in today. I'm her replacement." Johnny almost choking said good morning to her. As he took the coffee from her hands, he said, "Thank you. I am so glad you are here." As Johnny looked on his desk he saw a hand written letter that was neatly folded. The letter was from Sallie apologizing for her not being able to come to work today. A serious family matters had came up, and she would not be able to come in for weeks. She informed him that she would call him as soon as she could to give him an update. Johnny was saddened by this letter because he knew that Sallie would be at work if she could. He only prayed that everything was ok.

As he was thinking on the seriousness of Sallie's dilemma, the replacement secretary, with the sexy walk and smile, knocked on his office door. Johnny asked her to come in. He was still in deep thought about Sallie's troubles in her personal life. He wished he could take off himself to help her, but he knew that she would think it was too intruding for him to do so. Johnny did not like the fact that Sallie was so private with her personal life. Rosalyn said, "Good morning, Sir. I'm sorry I could not make it in at 9:00 sharp. The agency called me at 8:05, and I quickly prepared myself to come in as soon as I could. Please forgive me." Johnny thought to himself. How thoughtful she was to explain, especially since he was also late. He would not have known that she was late because she was already present when he had arrived.

Rosalyn was going toward his desk with her hand stretched out to shake his, when Johnny looked up and saw to his amazement, that she was the woman he had dreamed about just last night, the woman that had the sexy walk. Johnny again was very nervous. He often became nervous in the presence of beautiful women before the charismatic charm came flooding through. Johnny thought to himself, how he really wanted to meet this woman face to face, but he did not know that it was going to be so soon.

Rosalyn said to Johnny as he shook her outstretched hand, "Hi, my name is Rosalyn. I was sent here by the Mentors Secretarial Agency. I am a home interior decorator, but I work part time as an office assistant until my business grows and my reputation is widely known." Rosalyn was about to tell him her whole life story, but she stopped suddenly, recognizing that he might not want to hear all that. As he gathered his nerves, Johnny replied, "Hi, my name is Johnny Lambert. I am one of the executive building managers of this corporation, as well as the company's lawyer. It is so nice to meet you." They both smiled very warmly at each other.

The day went very well. They both seemed to feel at ease with each other after the initial tension broke. Rosalyn approached Johnny at the end of the day, and said, "It was a pleasure working with you today. I forgot to mention this, but a little while ago, the agency called and wanted me to inform you that your original secretary was not going to be in tomorrow and wondered could I come in for the rest of the week. I told them that I could, but I would have to talk to you to get your approval before I called them back to finalize the replacement."

Johnny responds, "Yes, of course. I would be honored if you could finish this week." All along he was growing more worried about Sallie because it was not like her not to call him and give him the update. Johnny knew that Sallie was a private woman and did not discuss her private life with anyone on her job, but he thought they were closer than what he had perceived. At least close enough that she would not have to go through a third party to relay a message to him when he felt like she could have easily picked up the phone and called him directly. Rosalyn said goodbye to Johnny, but he stayed a little while longer to finish his paper.

Chapter Five

As soon as he finished his paper work, he left the office and went to the Easy Meal diner. He knew that Linda was scheduled to work tonight. On Monday nights she always worked overtime. Johnny began to reminisce on how he had met Linda two years ago. He had the pleasure of laying eyes on a beautiful, tall slender young woman that was about twenty-six years old with dark black hair, high cheek bones, small straight nose, and beautiful slanted brown eyes. She also had a small oval face, and full lips. She was stunning, but tom boyish.

Johnny pursued her for at least six months before she gave him even a casual conversation. As with all tom boyish women he had met, they generally were harder to catch. In other words, he always had to put in extra time to get to know them. Besides, he found Linda to be utterly irresistible. Johnny walked into the diner, but Linda was nowhere to be found. He went to the front counter to ask Mrs. Lewis, the owner, was Linda coming in late? Mrs. Lewis informed Johnny that Linda had been in a terrible car accident, and she believed that she had to call her sister to come to take care of her.

Johnny asked Mrs. Lewis if she knew where Linda had recently moved to because she never got around to telling him her new address as she had intended too. He also had intended to tell Linda his new address, but because the two of them was always busy talking about other things, neither one of them was able to give the other one their new addresses. Mrs. Lewis said, "No, she failed to mention to me that she had moved, but if she calls, I will tell her that you would like to come by and check on her." Johnny said, "Thank you, Mrs. Lewis. Here is my cell number. If she does call, please call me with her new address." "I will, Johnny." said Mrs. Lewis.

Johnny left the Easy Meal diner and decided not to go out tonight. He was too worried about Linda and Sallie. He was very puzzled. It was not like either of them not to call him directly to let him know what was going on. Johnny thought to himself about how different the two women were from each other. Linda was so tom boyish and Sallie was so lady like. Both of them were so private, strong, and full of integrity. Johnny thought that must have been why he was so drawn to both of them.

As he pulled up into the parking lot of his apartment complex, he again noticed the small red Toyota car. He definitely wanted to pry and hang out in his car as long as it took, just to see if this car belonged to Sallie. He desperately wanted to find out if this was her. He missed her terribly, and wanted to know what was going on with her.

He walked onto his apartment and laid his suit jacket on his living room couch. Johnny took off his shoes, loosed his tie, and pulled his cell phone out of his pocket to call Linda. Linda answered the phone and said, "Hey Johnny, I was just about to call you. Mrs. Lewis told me you had just left the diner. I had called her to let her know that I was released from the hospital and my doctor took me off of work for several weeks to give my ® leg time to heal due to me breaking it when I was in the car wreck."

Johnny said, "Linda, are you alright? Why didn't you call me when you first had your car accident? I would have come to see about you and take care of you." Linda said, "I know Johnny. I was going to call you later on tonight when I thought you might be in from your fun with all of your lady friends. What are you doing home so early, anyway?" Johnny said, "I didn't go out tonight because I have been so worried about you. I thought we were better than this." Linda replied, "We are Johnny. I know you care about my well being. I would have called, but after the wreck, I was unconscious. All I know is that I woke up in the hospital and my sister was at my bedside. Whoever found me must have looked in my purse and found my sister's name and number in my wallet listed as my emergency contact. Will you forgive me?" Johnny said,

"Yes, I will forgive you, especially since you were in a serious car wreck, and you were unconscious. I only ask one thing. Please put me down as one of your emergency contacts. I don't know what I would do if I lost my little tom boyish friend. No matter how much you get on my nerves at times." Linda said, "No problem Johnny I will do anything for you. I know you love your best friend." Johnny said, "Yes, sometimes." He laughed out loud, and began to ask Linda for her new address. Linda told him.

Johnny excitedly said loudly, "Linda, do you know you live next door to me?" Linda replied, "No, I did not. I guess great minds think alike. How long have you been over this way?" Johnny informed her that he had only been at his new address for about a month. Linda told him she had only been at her new address for about two weeks.

Johnny said, "Linda, I have never noticed your car before." Linda said, "I can see why. By the time you leave the office and make it home from your nightly fun with your long list of fast women, you are so sleepy when you come home. All you can think of is your bed." Johnny said, "Yea, you probably are right. I guess I'm still looking for love in all the wrong places. I know I need to stop it, but right now, I'm still having too much fun. Besides, I'm looking for that special woman, since you want give me the time or day anymore."

Linda said, "Now Johnny, don't start that. You know what we agreed." Johnny said, "Alright, alright, I know you don't feel well, but I have to tell you this. You know that woman with the sexy walk that we were talking about in the diner." Linda said, "Yea, the woman you could not stop talking about." Johnny said, "Yea, that one. Well anyway. You will never believe how I met her." Linda said, "Johnny, please don't keep me in suspense. You are killing me. Tell me!"

Johnny replied, "This morning going into my office I was greeted with a beautiful smile that I thought was my secretary Sallie. I found out later, that it was not Sallie. It was the young woman with the sexy walk that I am so attracted to." Linda said, "Oh yea, that's great. You know Johnny my sister's name is Sallie." Johnny said, "No. I didn't know. You never told me that you had a sister. You only talked about how your parents died when you were sixteen, and your aunt and uncle raised you like their own. What is your sister's last name?" Linda said, "Sallie Long Heart. She was my father's first born through his first wife.

When my parents died in a plane crash, her mom came and got her. She and I were sixteen months apart. When I turned eighteen, I went looking for her. We have been together ever since." Johnny said, "You don't say. My secretary last name is Long Heart. Is she petite, slender, and have shoulder length sandy brown hair? Does she also have big round hazel eyes and full lips?"

Linda said, "Yea that is her. She has round hazel eyes like her mother, and we both have full lips like our father." Johnny said, "Small world. I thought that was her small red Toyota that I have been seeing for several nights parked at the curb in front of my apartment. Yea, now I am seeing how much you too are alike in the way you carry yourselves, and do not talk about your personal lives, but still yet so different in many ways. You are more adventurous than she is. She is more laid back and calm. You know how Christians act."

Linda said, "Yea Sallie is a Christian woman, but she can be quite adventurous when you get to know her. I guess because you two work together. At work, she tries to keep her relationships strictly professional. She is a hard case about those types of things. She despises office relationships. She believes, if you start any type of romantic relations, you can never go back to the way things were before."

Johnny said, jokingly, "Tell me about it. I found out the hard way." Linda said, "What you mean Johnny? Are you saying you are interested in my sister?" Johnny said, "Linda, let me let you go. I know you need your rest. Can I come to see you tomorrow?" Linda said, "Yes, Johnny, but call before you come. My schedule is very full. Tomorrow, I suppose to have an appointment with my doctor and start my physical therapy. I believe I am to be admitted into Friends Choice Home Health Company."

Johnny said, "Ok Linda. Get some rest, but before I let you go, have you ever mentioned me to Sallie?" Linda said, Yes, I told her about our relationship, but I never mentioned your name. She does not even know I know you. Johnny asked Linda to tell Sallie how the both of them knew each other. Eventually, how their romantic relationship ended in a lovely friendship due to the fact that the two of them agreed that they were more like sisters and brothers than a romantic couple. He also wanted Linda to tell Sallie to call him and give him and update on how she and Linda were doing on tomorrow.

Sallie did call Johnny the next morning after he had made it to the office. When he made it into the office Rosalyn was giving him the wireless phone letting him know it was Sallie. He noticed how Rosalyn was as prompt and beautiful as normal. They spoke to each other warmly as he walked into his office and began to talk with Sallie. "Sallie, how are you?"

Sallie replied, "Oh, I'm alright. I have been taking care of my sister. She told me how you two know each other. I'm sorry I did not call you directly. Everything was happening so fast. My sister and I have been there for one another as long as I can remember. I had to be with her when she needed me the most. I guess I was so worried about her, I was not thinking correctly. I mean, I know the Lord was there for her, but all I could think about was my little sister was almost taken away from me."

Johnny began to think about how strong Sallie's beliefs were as he replied, "Oh, Sallie, before I knew that something tragic had happened to Linda, I was worried about you, because I was so used to having you at work. However, when you called the agency to find you a replacement instead of calling me directly, I did not know what to think. You know how it is. We often think the worse before we think on the positive side of things. Thank God, your sister and I were so close, else I would not have found out what was going on with you, so soon." Sallie said, "Yes you would have. I would have called you. It was just that everything was going so fast. Please forgive me." Suddenly, the similarities of Linda and Sallie, was becoming even more apparent in their mannerism. Sallie said, "Ok, I will make sure I call you from here on out. Things are getting better since Linda is growing stronger.

Johnny, I need to be off for the next three weeks. Can you spare to be without me that long?" Johnny said, "I guess I can, but it will be hard to do without you that long. Rosalyn is a great secretary and person. I am finding that out more and more as we work together. Besides, it does not hurt that she is a striking beauty." Sallie said, "Alright Johnny. Slow your roll. Don't try to replace me while I'm out, just because I want agree to an office romance with you."

Johnny said, "Now, Sallie. How did you get all of that, out of the little that I just said?" Sallie said, "I know how to read between the lines." Johnny said, "No worries, Sallie. I would never jeopardize not being able to see you just because tragedy came into my two favorite women lives." Sallie said, "Ok, Johnny, don't let me have to remind you." Johnny said, "You won't have to." As they both begin to laugh out loud, they both said goodbye."

Johnny said to Sallie just as she left out the door, "Sallie, don't forget to tell my girl that I will stop by and see her if she is not too tired and I will bring your leave of absence paper work with me. Also if you are able to get them filled out and give them back to me, I will let you off a month to make sure your sister is alright and your pay will not be interrupted." She said, "Thanks Mr. Lambert. You are a good man. You will make somebody a good husband some day. Too bad things did not work out between you and my sister. She told me that your relationship was the best she had with a man but it felt more like you two were more like brother and sisters. She told me that you both still love each other, and are best friends."

Johnny said, "Yes, Linda is a great woman. I do still love her. She has all the qualities that I would want in a woman. She is down to earth, faithful, kind, strong, beautiful, and spiritual. I mean, I know, I don't talk about the Lord as much as I should, and I do things that are not in his will for my life by trying to find my own path, but I still believe in him." Sallie said, "Wow, I never heard you talk so openly about your beliefs before. That is a great thing for me to know about you. Let me run on. You know the two of us can talk all day, and before we know it, the day has passed by." Johnny said, "Ok Sallie, take it easy. I will be by later." "Ok, I will do that. We will be waiting on you."

Johnny called for Rosalyn. Rosalyn walked into Johnny's office. He notices she had a perfectly fitted two piece black suit that showed off her slender figure. All of her curves were in the right spots. She had her hair pulled up in the center, and the back hanging down. She wore glasses that made her look like a cross between a librarian and a business woman. It excited him every time he looked at her. He was beginning to think, how difficult it was going to be, to get his work done when she was just in the next office or in his presence.

He began to speak to her as he faced her sitting at his desk. "Rosalyn, how are you, today?" Rosalyn said, "I am doing well. I am glad to be here." Johnny thought to himself, Wow, she is sweet and sexy. Johnny said, "I'm glad you are here also. Speaking of that, Sallie my regular office assistant will be out on a leave of absence for a month, would you mind helping me until she is able to return." Rosalyn said, "Yes, I will be honored, but let me clear it with the agency first. Can I let you know by tomorrow morning?" Johnny said, "Yes. That will be cool." Johnny asked Rosalyn could she bring him a copy of the leave of absence paper work that was in the front office cabinet by the entrance of the office door.

Rosalyn told him that she would, as she walked out of his office to handle the task. Johnny watched her as she walked out and tried to maintain his thought processes, but he could not help himself. He signed to himself as he shook his head and said in a low voice, "My, my, my, Lord have mercy. Help me to maintain my professionalism when I am around her." He could not believe this beautiful creature was so near to him and would be working with him for a month. He was going to cherish the moments.

Johnny began to look over the project to build the apartment complexes in Phoenix, Arizona. He made a few phone calls and began to put the plans into operation. Although he tried to keep busy, he could not help but too think of his dear friend, Linda. He began to pray a compassionate prayer unto the Lord asking him to grant her a speedy recovery, and to bless her sister, Sallie, while she is by her bedside taking care of her.

Johnny knew that his weakness was women, but he wanted to do better. He always prayed for a good woman to help him to be more in the will of the Father, but the closest one to fit the prayer being answered, was Linda. Unfortunately, they round up being best friends instead of lovers. He also thought about how similar Linda and Sallie were, and that he would love to get to know her better. If only she would let her guards down.

He felt like Sallie would be perfect for him. She was strong, polite, independent, strikingly beautiful, spiritual, and had a quality of faithfulness and integrity that not many women possessed. The only other women that he seen those qualities in were his mother, sister, and Linda. Although, Johnny loved party girls because they seemed to be easier to talk to, he still admired women strong in their beliefs and did not have to have a man to take care of them. He loved their independence.

Rosalyn knocked on Johnny's door and waited until he asked her to enter. He told her to come in. She said, "Here is the leave of absence paperwork. Is there anything else you needed?" Johnny said, "No." Rosalyn began to tell Johnny that the agency said that it was ok for her to continue to work for him, and that he would have to fill out the necessary paperwork and turn it in to the agency. Johnny said, "Fine, just bring the paperwork when you get it."

Rosalyn said, "Mr. Lambert, do you remember when I told you that I only did this part time and that I was a home interior decorator." Johnny said, "Yes." Rosalyn continued, "If you have any future projects that you need someone to decorate, I hope you will keep me in mind. By the way, this morning when you were talking with Sallie, I received a phone call that was informing me that I had received a contract job to decorate some new buildings that are about to open in several months. They want me to start in a month. When Sallie comes back from her leave of absence, I will be starting on my short term position as an interior decorator with the contract job I mentioned earlier.

Johnny said, "That is great Rosalyn. I would love to help you celebrate your good fortune. Would you like to accompany me tonight when I go out dancing? Now, don't get me wrong, I am not coming on to you or anything. I just want to help you celebrate." Johnny knew he was telling one of those little white lies to cover up his real intentions. To his surprise, Rosalyn said, "Yes, I would love to go out with you to celebrate my good fortune." She also had a deep desire to go out with Johnny, but did not want to come across as forward.

Rosalyn was almost out of the office when she remembered that she already had plans. She began to tell Johnny, "Oh, Mr. Lambert, I am so sorry, but I almost forgot. I already have plans with my son." Johnny was surprised, "Wow, you have a son? I did not know you had a little boy. How old is he?"

Rosalyn told Johnny that her son was four years old, and he was a very smart young man. His father, her ex husband, was called out on business, and could not take him this weekend on his regularly scheduled visit. So, she told her son, Greg, Jr. that she would take him to see the Circus or to Chucky Cheese, so that he would not miss his dad so much. Johnny said, "Oh, you two are not together." Rosalyn said, "No we are not, but we still try to remain friends due to the fact we have a son together." Johnny said, "Ok, I understand that."

As Rosalyn walked out of the office, Johnny tried not to feel disappointed that she had a son. He often dreamt of the woman that he wanted to settle down with would not have any children. He wanted the woman he chose to be with to be childless as he was so they could start their family together. He did not know how he was to react to this. He had never pursued a woman that had children. As he processed this information, he decided that Rosalyn was worth it.

At the end of the day, Johnny and Rosalyn said their goodbyes. As he left the office, Johnny had the leave of absence paperwork in his hand to give to Sallie when he went to see his best girl, Linda. He also secretly, could not wait to see Sallie as well.

CHAPTER SIX

JOHNNY PULLED INTO his driveway and went into his apartment to take a quick shower before he went over to Linda's house. When he was just about to walk outside, his phone rang. He picked up the phone and said, "Hello." It was Sallie on the phone saying, "Mr. Lambert, I know you had said you were coming by, but after a long day with the Physical Therapist, Linda finally fell asleep. She has been having trouble sleeping in the day and the night. Bless her heart. She has been working so hard with the nurses and the therapists that she has worn herself out."

Johnny said, "Ok, I understand. I just looked forward to seeing her tonight. Well, anyway, Sallie, I brought the leave of absence paperwork home to give to you so that you can fill them out. If you finish them tonight I can turn them in tomorrow, so that your pay will not be interrupted. I will give them to you, later, I guess." Sallie said, "Oh, Thank you so much, Mr. Lambert. If it is alright, can I come over to your apartment to fill out the paperwork in about thirty minutes so that I want wake Linda?" Johnny said, "Of course. I would love for you to come by."

Sallie fixed a sandwich plate and set it on the table where Linda could easily reach it, if she woke up and was hungry. It was already some orange juice and water on the table that could easily be reached by Linda if she needed it. In the meantime, Johnny cooked some spaghetti and meatballs and baked some garlic bread. He tossed a salad and put all of it on the dining room table. He also pulled out some fresh wine and then put it back because he did not want to offend Sallie if she did not drink wine. He made some lemon tea, instead. Johnny even lit some candles to set a romantic tone. He often did this type of thing, so that he could relax, after a long day of work. Plus he wanted to impress Sallie, and try to get her to sit and eat with him.

Johnny began to think about how he would have to prepare to leave in about six weeks to go to Orlando, Florida to head the Penn Hotel project. As he sat down in deep thought of this, the doorbell rang. Johnny got up to answer it. It was Sallie. She was in some nicely fitted designer jeans with a red fancy silk shirt that made her look like a beautiful little teenage girl. Johnny had never seen Sallie look so casual. She looked teen years younger. Face it, Johnny felt like he had hit the jackpot in being friends with such beautiful sisters. He invited Sallie to sit at the table where he had placed the leave of absence paperwork and invited her to join him in eating the food he had prepared.

As they set down and ate. They talked about how they grew up, and their likes and dislikes. What they liked in the opposite sex, and what their future goals were. Sallie said to Johnny, "Mr. Lambert, I never knew this about you." Johnny said, "Sallie, please call me Johnny. We know each other outside the office, and we don't have to be so formal."

Sallie asked, "How can two people work together, for six years and know so little about each other?" Johnny said, "Well, Sallie, I tried to get to know you better, but you made sure you put a stop to that notion, just when I thought I was getting close to you. I know you do not care for office romances, but I promise you, it would be so much more than that to me. You would be so much more." Sallie replied, "Sure, I was against office romances, but not office friendships, just as long as it would not have interfered with our professional working relationship. I have seen a lot of office relationships go bad, never to recover a professional working environment. That is why I am so against them."

Johnny said, "Ok, I'm with you. Maybe it is just as well, but again, Sallie, all I wanted to do was get to know you better. We are so busy at work that we don't really have a chance to talk, like we are doing now.

Sallie, while you are on a leave of absence, I would love to see where our friendship could lead us." Sallie said. "Ok, we will see." Sallie finished filling out the rest of the leave of absence paperwork and handed them to Johnny, and told him that she was sorry, but she had to get back to Linda. Sallie said, "Thank you for the dinner. It was very nice. I will tell Linda that you wanted to stop by, but she was asleep." Johnny said, "Ok, tell her that if all goes well, that I will be by tomorrow."

Sallie said, "Johnny that would be great. Could you come by around 6:00 pm? There is a church program that I want to go to tomorrow night. Johnny, was up with you anyway? You have not been going out as much as you used to. Are you sick, worried, or tired? Johnny answered her sarcastically, "To answer the first question, I will be glad to stay with Linda tomorrow. I miss being with her. To answer your second question, I am becoming tired of going out partying so much. I am also getting tired of party girls. Besides, I'm thinking about settling down."

Sallie said, "Good. It is about time you started thinking about settling down. You know you are not a young teenager anymore. Your lack of sleep and lack of rest is starting to show. Yea, I see those little wrinkles on your forehead." Johnny began to laugh out loud. Sallie continued to tease Johnny, "All those women that you are dating are most likely starting to stress you out. I will tell Linda that you will be there tomorrow to sit with her while I go to church."

Johnny replied as he was laughing, "Whatever, you got jokes. I will see you tomorrow." Sallie said, "Alright Mr. Lambert, you have a good evening. I hope to see you tomorrow." Johnny insisted that she call him Johnny, even after, she returned to work. Sallie often referred to Johnny as Mr. Lambert because she wanted to always put a wall between them so that they would keep their office working relationship from becoming too personal.

Chapter Seven

Johnny arrived at work tomorrow a little earlier than usual the next day. He was trying to set a good example. As he was driving he began to think about Sallie and how he enjoyed talking to her last night at his apartment. He also began to think about Linda and the tragic car wreck she had been involved in. He did not know what he would do if he lost his best friend. He and Rosalyn became closer, and worked very well together. He sought after ideas, how he could ask her out again, without it sounding or being unprofessional. Johnny turned in Sallie leave of absence paper work to the Human Resources department so that her pay checks would continue to flow without hesitation.

At the end of the day, Rosalyn walked into Johnny's office, and asked him, did he need anything before she left for the day. Johnny said, "Yes, would you like to go out with me tonight about 9:00 pm. We never got a chance to celebrate you landing that contract job for interior decorating." Rosalyn said, "Yes, I would love to." She was almost surprised that she had answered so quickly, but she was hoping that he would ask her out again. She just did not know it was going to be so soon.

Johnny had asked her to meet him at his house. Rosalyn asked Johnny to give her his address. He did so, and told her he looked forward to seeing her tonight. He had also given her his cell phone number in case she had any trouble finding his apartment. Rosalyn left the office feeling so excited. She thought it was nice to get to know a man that appeared to be a good man and trustworthy. Johnny stayed at the office a little longer and went home.

As Johnny was pulling into his driveway, he noticed Sallie's small red Toyota car. That is when he realized that he had told Sallie that he would sit with Linda tonight while she went to church. He shook his head in distress because he forgot to get Rosalyn's telephone number just in case something came up. He decided to let things work itself out. He only hoped for the best. Johnny took a quick shower, changed clothes, and quickly went to Linda's apartment. Johnny rang the doorbell. Sallie came quickly, to open the front door. She was running late. They spoke teasingly to one another. After last night, they both felt very comfortable around each other.

On her way out, Sallie told Johnny that Linda was in her bedroom down the hallway to the right, and told him that she would be back by 9:00pm. Johnny was relieved when she said 9:00 pm because he remembered the plans he had made with Rosalyn. He thought to himself, since Sallie mentioned that she would be back at 9:00 pm, there was no need for him to tell her about his plans with Rosalyn at 9:00pm. Sallie was always a timely woman. Johnny called out Linda's name before he entered her room. Linda was very happy to see him. They talked about her recovery, Rosalyn, and the nice dinner he and Sallie had last night when she was over to his apartment finishing up the leave of absence paperwork.

Linda was happy that Johnny and Sallie were getting along so well together. She was also happy that Johnny was finally pursuing a woman that was not so fast, and seemed more settled. Johnny told Linda that Rosalyn had a little boy whom she was devoted to, and did not have time to get out much. To be honest, Linda felt more comfortable with the idea of Johnny being with her sister, Sallie, rather than with Rosalyn. She did not know why he seemed so crazy about a woman he hardly knew, especially a woman that had a child. He does not usually pursue women with children.

The time was passing quite fast, before he knew it, it was 9:00 pm. Johnny had informed Linda how he had invited Rosalyn over to his apartment at 9:00 pm, and had forgot about he had already told Sallie that he would sit with her tonight. He begged her for forgiveness. She forgave him, because she knew that Johnny was a good man.

However, when it came to the women that he pursued, he did not think with his head on his shoulders. He thought with his other brain. Basically, he did not think at all when it came to him and any beautiful woman he was interested in. Linda told Johnny she was a big girl, and that she did not need a baby sitter. Johnny excused himself, and headed toward his apartments. Rosalyn had just pulled up, when he was about to open his front door.

Johnny turned around to greet Rosalyn, "Hello Rosalyn. I had just made it home. I was over to one of my friend's house. She had a wreck last week. When I asked you out tonight, I had forgot I told Sallie, her sister, that I would sit with Linda, while she went to church tonight. I told Linda about what I did and begged her forgiveness. She told me that she was a big girl and did not need anyone to baby sit her. I told her that I was coming over to meet you and that I would be back. Would you like to meet her?" Rosalyn said, "Sure, I want to meet all the other women in your life because I don't want any friction between your old friends, and your new ones, like me." Johnny said, "I heard that. Well, come on. Let us go over there."

As Johnny and Rosalyn approached Linda's door, he rang the doorbell as he and Rosalyn walked into the apartment. Johnny said, "Linda it is Rosalyn and I. I am bringing Rosalyn into your bedroom so she can meet you." Linda said, "Ok, You both come on in." Linda was in her bed lying down. Rosalyn was surprised how beautiful Linda was. She also was surprised how much Linda and Sallie favored. Johnny had told her that Sallie, his secretary, was Linda's sister, and how he had just found about it, while they walked from his apartment to Linda's apartment. Johnny said, "Linda this is Rosalyn. Rosalyn this is Linda, my best friend."

Rosalyn and Linda spoke to each other and talked casually a little while together. Johnny said to Linda, "Linda, Sallie said she was going to be back at 9:00 pm and it is already 9:20pm." Linda said, "Yes, Johnny, but if Sallie is late you know it has to be a good reason behind it."Just as Linda had finished saying those words, the phone began to ring. Linda said, "Johnny will you please answer the phone." Johnny answered the phone. It was Sallie explaining why she was late, and could not call any sooner. A lady at the church experienced a diabetic crisis, and 911 had to be called. Sallie told Johnny that the woman was fine, and she was on her way to the ER. She told Johnny that she was leaving the church now and on her way home. She promised that she would try to be there by 10:00 pm. Johnny told Linda and Rosalyn about what had happened with Sallie.

Johnny apologized to Rosalyn for them not being able to go out dancing as they had planned, and that he had told Sallie that he would stay with Linda until she was able to get here. Rosalyn told him that was fine because Greg Jr. was with his father. He had told her that he would keep Greg, Jr. for the next few days for she could rest and do some of the things she wanted to do. Johnny and Linda were amazed about how sensitive Rosalyn's ex husband was to Rosalyn's and their son's needs. Rosalyn asked Linda and Johnny could she stay with them until Sallie showed up. They both said to her, "Sure, you can."

Rosalyn was beginning to love working with Johnny and she wanted to get to know him a little better, outside of work. Besides, she wanted to size up the competition and get a glimpse of just how close Sallie, Linda, and Johnny's relationship was really like. Johnny did not know how Rosalyn was known to eliminate her competitors, but she knew that she had her work cut out if she was even going to attempt to eliminate Linda and Sallie from being so attached to them.

She decided not to pursue this, at this time, because the bond between Linda and Johnny already seemed unbreakable by just the little time she witnessed them two together. She also saw that Linda and Johnny's relationship was not sexual, but yet a very close friendship, almost like real brothers and sisters.

Sallie made it back to Linda's apartment at 9:50 pm. Johnny met her at the door. He apologized about how he had forgotten about staying with Linda tonight and had asked Rosalyn to go out with him tonight. Sallie was surprised how Johnny had met her at the door with this. She was equally surprised on how soon Johnny had already asked Rosalyn out, but she tried not to focus on it. She and Rosalyn spoke to each other, politely. Rosalyn looked at Sallie. Sallie looked so much younger than the first time she met her at the office. She was very petite and beautiful. On the other hand, Linda was tall and had a lean model type body. She could tell they were sisters. They both had the same full lips they had inherited from their father.

Not soon after Sallie arrived, she noticed how well Johnny and Sallie was at ease with each other, and their ability to talk and tease each other as if no one was in the room besides the two of them. Linda watched them in amazement, and was happy to see the two of them getting along so well. She often wanted the best for them both, and what greater joy she would have, if the two of them round up together as a couple. Rosalyn also noticed how close Sallie and Johnny were, but she felt a little intimidated.

Johnny finally looked at Rosalyn and realized that this night was about not only being with close friends, but also with the woman he had invited to spend the evening with him. He turned around and gave her the type of look that a woman would know that the guy was only interested in her. He began to talk to her very softly, "I'm sorry Rosalyn. I am caring on like you are not even in the room."

Rosalyn said, "Yea, I wondered had you noticed that?" Johnny knowing all the time that when it came to Sallie or Linda he was like that, but he did not want to make Rosalyn upset, when he was trying to get to know her better. He asked her was she ready to go. She told him, yes, she was. So they said goodbye to Linda and Sallie and walked over to his apartment.

Chapter Eight

After Johnny and Rosalyn had left, Linda began to tease Sallie on how her and Johnny was carrying on like no one else was in the room but them, and how Rosalyn noticed what was going on between the two of them, and had this puzzled look on her face. Linda said to Sallie, " She clearly figured out that witnessing Johnny and I together that we had an unbreakable bond but there was no romance going on, but with the two of you, I don't know if she felt threatened or intimidated. You two were so comfortable with each other, and it was clearly noticeable. She did not want you to steal her man. Can you blame her, Johnny is a catch."

Sallie said to Linda, "Linda, you don't have anything to worry about concerning Johnny and I. He is my boss. We are comfortable with each other because of all those years we have been working together." Linda said, "Ok Sallie don't let a good man pass you by, while you are waiting for that perfect man that is sinless, to come forth." They both started laughing as they kissed each other on the cheek and went to bed.

As Johnny and Rosalyn walked into his apartment, he asked Rosalyn to make herself comfortable. Johnny put on some slow romantic music from his Luther Van dross collection. He came back over to the couch she was sitting on, and looked at her beautiful black eyes, and said to her with a soft seductive voice, "Rosalyn, you look so amazingly beautiful. I have been dreaming of this moment from the first time I saw you in garage parking lot. You did not notice me, but I sure noticed you. I kept saying to myself, who is this beautiful person that has graced my world with her beauty. It is like you was one of the angels that had accidently fallen from the heavenly pearly gates. I could not help but say to God, "Thank you for making a beautiful angel like this."

Rosalyn was melting as he spoke to her. She could hear his soft panting breathing as he spoke sexy and romantic words to her. He moved closer to her body, and leaned over and kissed her very softly and with such romantic hunger that she almost fainted with blissful pleasure. He slowly leaned his body over hers being very mindful not to offend her with his advances. As he noticed her responding to him, he began to caress her all over her body, slowly, then with moderate intensity. Rosalyn sighed with pleasure.

She could not believe how romantic he was. He really knew how to make a woman feel so, so good. Johnny reached over to grab Rosalyn's hands to bring her closer to him. He pulled her face to his, and looked into her eyes while he was slightly moistening his lips. He whispered in her ear, "Rosalyn, we don't have to go out tonight if you don't want to." I would like us to spend a romantic evening here, if you so desire." Rosalyn could do nothing but nod her head, yes, as she followed him into his master bedroom as he guided her by her hand.

When they entered his bedroom, he picked her up, and laid her on his bed. He carefully pulled off her shirt and began to softly caress her wonderful, bouncy, round breast. He began to softly kiss her breast with his lips. He caressed her nipple with his tongue. He moved down to her waist, as he kissed her beautiful little curvy body. He unbuttoned her jeans and pulled her jeans down as he leaned over her body. Finally, he took off his clothes.

He again began to kiss Rosalyn on her lips, and softly caressed her tongue with his. Johnny asked Rosalyn, softly, "Do you like how I am making you feel?" Rosalyn could only sign with complete pleasure. Johnny kissed her stomach, and then her inner thighs, and carefully entered her with excited passion. He slowly began to move while inside her, making sure she felt comfortable. When he knew that she was ready for more intensity, he begin to move faster and faster, and then slowed down, to make sure he did not overwhelm her.

He kissed her passionately so that she could enjoy every part of their sexual encounter. Johnny began to kiss her deeply and move in her deeper and faster, until both of their bodies were synchronized with so much burning love that it was almost impossible to stand. Then suddenly both of them climaxed with such fulfillment that both of them screamed out, yes, yes, yes.......from the exciting pleasure. Johnny kissed Rosalyn's forehead, and said, "My, my, my, you are a little fireball aren't you?" Rosalyn looked at him and smiled. She could not believe what had just occurred, and how good.............it felt. She wanted more, but she did not want to appear too forward.

She asked Johnny could he excuse her, as she got up to freshen up a bit. Johnny asked her was she hungry because he could fix her something to eat or take her out. It was her choice. Rosalyn came out of the bathroom very refreshed as she pulled her hair up in a bun. She looked so beautiful. Johnny could not help but pull her close to him and give her a passionate kiss. He said to her, "Rosalyn, you are a dream. Are you hungry? Would you like for me to fix you something to eat or would you like me to take you out to your favorite eating place? As for me, my hunger has been fulfilled, but I would love to have the luscious snack of having you in my arms all night long." Rosalyn said, "Johnny, you are too much. Where did you learn how to pleasure a woman like that?"

Johnny voiced, "It was not something that I studied. I guess it was a learned trait. My father is always very affectionate toward my mother, not only in the presence of my brother, sister, and I, but in the presence of every one. He makes sure that my mother is not a dissatisfied married woman that does know that she is richly loved. He wants the world to know how much he loves his sweet maple Bell. That is my father's pet name for my mother. Her name is Bell."

Rosalyn said, "Oh Johnny, I would love to stay here all night with you, but I can't. Can we do this again, really soon. I have to meet Greg, Jr. and his dad tomorrow afternoon at the circus. Greg, Jr. begged me to come with them. I could not say no." Johnny looked at her, and again could not believe he was dating a woman that had a child, but after tonight, he knew that she was worth it.

He walked her to her car and kissed her very softly with longing desire to be intimate with her again. He really did not want to let her go, but he knew that she had other responsibilities to handle. She drove off slowly. Johnny watched her as she pulled off, until he could no longer see her car. He walked back to his apartment, and turned off Luther Van dross' classic CD album. He walked into his bedroom and dreamed about the romantic sexual encounter that he had with Rosalyn. He slept like a baby. He could not help it. She was just that sweet.

Saturday morning Johnny woke up with a brand new spirit of joy. He went into his kitchen and cooked himself several pancakes, three pieces of bacon and two scrambled eggs. He poured himself a glass of orange juice and sat down and ate his breakfast. He thought on the enjoyable night he had with Rosalyn. He also was slightly disturbed about Rosalyn was still spending a lot of time with her ex husband, not to mention, how they were spending time as a family. He tried not to ponder on it, but at times, he could not help himself.

Suddenly, the phone rang. He reached over to get it. He said, "Hello, this is Johnny." Sally was on the line and began to speak, "Mr. Lambert, I mean, Johnny, I need to run to the store. Could you come over and keep Linda, company, while I am gone. Linda told me that she was not a baby, and she could take care of herself, but I know Ms. Independence, she would overdue it and reinjure her knee." Johnny of course said he would come over anytime, and that he was planning on coming over today anyway, to visit them. Sallie said, "Great, when can you come?" Johnny said, "I will be over in about thirty minutes. Is that alright?" Sallie replied, "Yes, that is fine. Thank you, Johnny."

Johnny finished his breakfast took a shower and put on some blue jeans and a nice sport shirt that matched his eyes, and left his apartment to go over to Linda's apartment. He rang the door bell. Sallie met him at the door. She had a beautiful sea blue dress on, and her hair twisted up in the front as the back of hair flowed downward. Wow, his breath was almost taken away, when he laid eyes on her, but he tried to contain himself. Sallie said, "Hey Johnny, thank you for coming with such short notice. I am glad to see you. You are looking very sporty and handsome." Johnny laughed and said, "Not half as good as you are looking. Sallie, my, my, my, you are definitely looking good." Sallie told Johnny she would be back as soon as she could.

Johnny walked back to Linda's den. Linda looked amazing as she always did with her beautiful black hair that always was long, straight, and shiny. He said to her, "Have you been over doing it?" She said, "No, I heard Sallie telling you that I was. She can't help herself. She is very over protective when it comes to me." Johnny said, "Yes, I have come to know that." Linda said, "So how is Rosalyn doing?" Johnny said, very softly, "She is doing wonderful. She should be with her son and her ex husband at the circus by now."

Linda looked into Johnny's eyes and face, as he spoke. She could not believe that her dear friend was falling for a woman that had not only a child, but also an ex-husband that seemed to always be very near Rosalyn. She knew that Johnny was getting involved with a love triangle, but she wanted him to enjoy her as long as he could. However, she did tell Johnny to be very careful. They begin to laugh and talk about other things. The two of them could always engage in some adventurous topics.

Chapter Nine

While Sallie was shopping, trying to reach an item on a top shelf, a handsome, tall slender man with perfect muscular tone, blonde hair, and crystal blue eyes noticed her inability to reach the item. He reached up and asked her, "Is this it?" She blushed and said, "Yes, that is it." He said, "Hi, my name is Jeffery." Sallie told him her name. They talked a little as she finished shopping. She felt at ease with him. He asked Sallie if he could have her number and call her sometime. Sallie told him she did not give out her number to people she just met, but if he wanted to give her his number, she would more than likely call him one day.

As Sallie was leaving the store, Jeffery asked Sallie could she call him Monday evening about 6:00 pm, giving him time to make it home from work. He was a lawyer at the Johnson and Johnson law firm. One of the biggest law firms in Phoenix, Arizona. Sallie told him that she would. Sallie made it back to her sister's apartment. She walked in on Linda and Johnny laughing, talking, and joking with each other. Johnny asked her did she need any help putting the groceries away. She said, "No thanks, I have already received enough help for today, to last me for about a week." Johnny and Linda looked at each other.

Linda asked Sallie what went on at the grocery store, and why was she having such a pleasant smile on her face. She looked at them both and said, "I met a man." As she screamed it out loud. Linda said, "What, you met a man at the grocery store? I have been looking for one just to talk to." Johnny looked at Linda saying, "What am I, chopped liver?" Linda said, "Of course not. You are my sweetie, my night and shining armor, and like my brother, but I am thinking about settling down and getting married. I want to have kids before I turn thirty. So that I can still run and play with them." Johnny said, "Alright Linda, whatever you say."

He was happy to hear Linda say those words. He was thinking along the same lines. He asked Sallie about the man she had met. He felt a little jealous because she spoke so well of a man she had just met. He asked her, "So, when are we going to meet this man?" Sallie said, "Before, I bring him around my family and friends, I first have to get to know him a little myself."

Johnny just looked at her with pain in his eyes. He was the one so desperately trying to get to know Sallie a little better. He thought he was finally going to have the chance to do so, while she was out on leave of absence. He thought to himself how selfish he was being, after all, he was now dating Rosalyn whom he adored. He said to himself, Sallie deserves a chance to have a man in her life, but he was going to make sure that this Jeffery was the man for her. He had already determined that both Sallie and Linda deserved the best.

Sallie made Italian pasta and meatballs, baked some Italian bread, and fixed some asparagus sticks with romaine lettuce for dinner. She asked Johnny if he would stay and have dinner with her and Linda. He said he would enjoy that very much. They laughed and talked all that night. Johnny got so close with the two of them that he wished he could make this a daily routine. They were less complicated than the other women that he had been involved with.

He finally had to call it a night. It was already late, almost 1:00am. Once he made it home, he checked his messages. He noticed that Rosalyn had called him and wanted to know if she could come over tomorrow to spend some time with him. He forgot that he had given her his home number. She must have misplaced his cell number. He made a note to call her in the morning. He had already promised Sallie and Linda that he would visit their church tomorrow. He would call her after services. He laid on his couch and fell fast to sleep.

He woke up about 9:00am. He put on his navy blue Armani suit with his gold toned navy Stacy Adams shoes. He also topped it off with a white long sleeve shirt with a grey, yellowish, navy tinged tie. He called Linda's house to see if they were ready. They all met at Johnny's car. His car was the largest out of the three cars so he volunteered to drive them to church so that Linda could ride in comfort. She had already missed three Sunday services since she injured her leg in the car wreck.

When Linda and Sallie saw Johnny both of them were very proud to be seen with him. They both thought and told him he looked like a male model that was in a DQ Fashion magazine. Linda and Sallie both said, "Johnny, you are looking so fine." He smiled and said as he always did about the two of them, "I must be the most blessed man in the world to be in the company of two of the most beautiful women in the world." Both Linda and Sallie could not resist teasing him by saying, "You mean besides Rosalyn."

He blew them off by saying, "Right now it is all about you two. Rosalyn is beautiful like an angel, but right now, it is all about the two of you." They both said, "Whatever, Mr. Charmer. You could almost talk your way into getting whatever you wanted." Johnny looked straight at Sallie and replied, "No, not everything." I have not had that pleasure yet. I'm still working on it." Sallie blushed and quickly changed the subject, by saying, "Come on Johnny let us get focused on the Lord, after all this is the day that the Lord has made. We should rejoice and be glad in it." Johnny said, "Alright Ms. Missionary. I hear you."

They made it to church about 10:55am. The Pastor talked about strange affairs that people have in the world with different things and different people, trying to find out their real purpose for life. He really brought that message out. At first, Johnny, thought the preacher was talking directly to him, but then he realized what he already knew from his youth, that God knows, everything about us. There is nothing that he doesn't know, nor sees. After church services were over, Johnny hugged some of the members and all three of them left together to go home.

They did not want to wear Linda out so they agreed not to go out to eat. Sallie volunteered to cook Sunday dinner for them. Johnny was asked to join them, but he declined the invitation and told them that he had something to take care of. He kissed them both on their cheek and the three departed in to their homes.

Sallie cooked a beautiful tasty roast, homemade mashed potatoes with gravy sauce, green beans, and buttery rolls. She also made some raspberry tea. Johnny hurriedly called Rosalyn once he had made it to his apartment. He told her that he would love for her to come over this evening, and that he would take her out to dinner, since they did not make it there the other night. Johnny changed his clothes and put on some of his slow jams.

The door rang. Johnny answered the door. It was Sallie she had brought him a plate of the food she had cooked. He was surprised to see her. He invited her in and said, "Sallie you did not have to do this." She replied, "I know. I did not want you to starve or anything." Johnny said to her teasingly, "Yea, right. Sallie, you know you came over here just because you wanted to see me."

Sallie replied while laughing out loud, "Only you would say something like that, but I do want to tell you how fine you were looking earlier today. Now, don't get the wrong ideal. I am not trying to get with you or anything like that." Johnny said, "Ok Sallie, whatever you say." Sallie said, "Well let me go before you start thinking I want you or something." They both laughed. Johnny thanked Sallie for bringing him a plate of food and for thinking about him.

Just as Sallie was entering Linda's apartment, Rosalyn pulls up. Rosalyn gets out and walks toward Johnny's apartment and began to ring Johnny's doorbell. She notices Sallie as she entered into Linda's apartment, but could not speak because Sallie already had her back turned going in. Johnny opened his door, and saw a beautiful vision. Rosalyn had her beautiful shining straight hair flowing down her back. She had on a pink shirt with a blue jean skirt. She also had a beautiful loose designer belt on to accent her outfit very well. She was a beautiful vision.

Johnny asked Rosalyn was she ready to go. She said, "Yes, I am hungry." Johnny said, "Where ever you want to go, I'm ready. It is my treat." Rosalyn replied, "Well, there was a little romantic Italian restaurant just right down the road from your house. There are always a lot of cars in their parking lot." Johnny said, "Well, let us go before they become to full."

They left. He drove them in his car. Johnny and Rosalyn made it to La Roman Italian Restaurant safely. He opened the door for her and they walk inside the restaurant together. They were seated in the back at a table that had candle lights with fresh roses on their table that accented the whole restaurant. Candle light dinners really set the tone for romance. They ordered their meals, and surprisingly, it arrived soon after. They laughed and talked about different things that interested them, and they both found out how much they had in common.

Johnny looked into Rosalyn eyes as he moistened his lips. He said to her in a cool romantic voice, "Rosalyn you look very sexy tonight." He reached over and touched her hands that were under the table. Rosalyn felt electricity run throughout her body, as he touched her. As he continued to talk romantically to her in his masculine voice, Rosalyn began to melt in her seat. Johnny said, "Rosalyn you look so good and smell so sweet that I can drink your bath water. Rosalyn thought to herself, now, why did he have to go there. She began to squirm in her seat. She was suddenly getting so hot, but tried so desperately to stay cool.

After all, they were in a public place. Rosalyn finally managed to say something, "Johnny you don't look bad yourself. I must say, I appreciate a man that knows how to talk to a woman to make her feel like she is the only woman he desires to be with. You must have had a lot of practice. You really know how to pour it on."

She noticed he had a white sports shirt on with some black casual dress pants that really accented his muscular body. Johnny said, "Well Rosalyn, right now, you are setting my whole world on fire. I can hardly contain my desire for you. Are you ready to get out of here?" She hurriedly said, "Yes, after all, I have already made a fool out of myself, squirming in this chair as you spoke those words to me, and I am not usually like this. I don't know what to say about how you make me feel in your presence. Especially, when you talk and look at me with so much desire."

Johnny said to Rosalyn, "Rosalyn right now my mind is not on food any more. It is strictly on taking you back to my place, so that I can be alone with you." Rosalyn said, "Johnny we had better leave now, because you got me so stirred up. I can hardly sit still. Johnny walked over to Rosalyn and pulled her chair out so that she could easily stand up. He left the money on the table for the meal and the tip for the waiter, and they hurriedly left the restaurant and made it to Johnny's apartment in record time.

Johnny walked over to the passenger door and let Rosalyn get out of the car before he grabbed her hand in his, and led her into his apartment. Before they could get into the door, he leaned over and began to passionately kiss Rosalyn soft, moist lips. He said to himself, ooh she tastes so good. He deepened the kiss as he began to lift her shirt off of her body. He also took off his shirt. He began to loosen his pants, and let them flow from his body as he stepped out of them.

He began to unbutton her jean skirt, as he loosened her belt. The belt and the skirt fell to the floor. He picked her up in his arms as he took her over to his spacious couch. He decided that the space that he needed was not going to be large enough for what he wanted to do with Rosalyn. He picked her up again, as he continued to kiss her deeply, passionately, with so much hot lustful sensation. Electric currents were going throughout both of their bodies. They were both on fire for each other.

Johnny and Rosalyn passionately released themselves to all the acts of love they felt like exploring as the bed rocked back and forth in motion with their bodies as they built up tempo until both of them climaxed into pure pleasure. Johnny asked her to stay the night, but she said she could not because she did not bring any extra clothes even though she knew her ex husband still had her their son, Greg Jr. at his place.

She asked to use his bathroom so that she could freshen up. As she was leaving, she kissed Johnny's moist warm lips that stilled burned with heat from their love making. Johnny pulled her close to him, still ready to go another round, as he tried to get her to stay. She was very tempted to stay, but she knew it would look very awkward if she showed up at the office in casual clothes and not a business suit as she was so accustomed to wearing. She left as they both said good bye and drove home. After all that great love making, they both fell fast asleep and slept through the night without getting up.

Chapter Ten

They both made it to work on time, and tried to maintain a professional relationship in spite of what happened between the two of them this weekend. They still enjoyed each other, but kept everything low keyed, so that the other office employees could not tell that they were seeing each other outside of work. They went on like this over the next two to three weeks until the final week in which Rosalyn was due to leave and Sallie was due to come back. Johnny and Rosalyn came together once more in sexual bliss before her final week was up. The final week that Rosalyn would leave and Sallie would come back.

On Friday Sallie came to the office to make sure everything was in place. It was about 11:00, when she stopped by the office. Johnny was overjoyed to see Sallie. He had not seen her since she had brought him the plate of food she had cooked the Sunday he had went to church with her and Linda. He and Sallie were shooting the breeze, laughing, and talking like they always did, as if no one else was in the room. Of course Rosalyn took notice of it, and became moved with indignation. She made it known to Johnny that she was present and she knew that he had an uncanny way of tuning everybody else out when Sallie was in room.

She called Johnny in his office so she could let him know just how obvious it is that he had a thing for Sallie. She felt like a fool not to notice, just how close they were, until now. Johnny tried to play it off because he also had serious feelings for Rosalyn. He was drawn between two different women, and he knew it. Johnny was not trying to make his feeling of Sallie so obvious, but apparently, he was failing at trying to keep it all to himself. He tried to calm Rosalyn down, by assuring her that he only had eyes for her, but she was not buying it. Rosalyn gave up, because it was obvious whatever he had for Sallie, she was going to have a time, getting him to drop those feelings, and have him concentrating only on her.

Rosalyn left Johnny in his office standing alone, wondering what just happened. Sallie noticed that something was wrong especially when Johnny came out of his office with an odd look on his face. Sallie voiced, "Johnny it is obvious that I came by at an inconvenient time. Please excuse me. Rosalyn, I apologize for just showing up unannounced, but I was just trying to see if everything was going ok. I had not talk to Johnny in two weeks because I knew that he has been busy. I was going to see what his plans were for next week because I knew it was almost time for him to go Orlando, Florida to help them put the final touches on the Penn Hotel project."

Rosalyn looked at Johnny because he had failed to mention that the date for him to go was soon approaching. Johnny noticed the confused look on Rosalyn face. He calmly answered Sallie and told her that it would be the Monday after she comes back when he would be preparing to go. He walked Sallie out because he wanted to know how her and that young man she met at the grocery store was coming along. Sallie told him that they were officially dating now, and that he was a very nice man.

Johnny asked her was he a Christian man because he did not want her to lessen her standards, just to be with a man. Sallie told him that as of now, he says he is a Christian. He knows that I am, because he has already attempted to take our relationship to the next level, and I have not let it go there because I am saving myself for the one I will marry, no matter how much I'm drawn to him. Johnny felt good when he heard her say those words.

He teased her in saying, "Yea, you better be saving yourself for me. You know that I am your future husband." He laughed and said, "Sallie, you know I am teasing you." He knew that he would love to have that chance to get to know her better, but right now, he respected the idea that he was with Rosalyn. Sallie said, "Ok Johnny, you should go back inside before Rosalyn becomes more upset with you. I see how close you two have become. I just hope it lasts even when she is no longer working here." Johnny said, "I hope so too. Pray for us."

Sallie leaves, and Johnny goes back into the office. Rosalyn of course is upset, and Johnny knew she had a right to be. He tried to calm her down, and assure her that there was nothing going on between him and Sallie, but Rosalyn was not buying it. It was too obvious. She began to let him know just how she felt, "Johnny do you know that when Sallie comes around, you act like you and her are the only two people in the room. Now, it is one thing if other people see what is going on, and it is another thing, if your girlfriend is present and she sees it. I don't think you realize how much you have a thing for Sallie. It is so obvious Johnny that your feelings for her are very strong."

Johnny began to talk softly to Rosalyn, "Rosalyn, I admit that Sallie is a great friend of mine. She has been my administrative assistant for about six years. She and I know each other very well, but there is nothing romantic going on between the two of us. I admit, when the two of us, initially started working together, I tried to get her to go out with me. Sallie shut that down quickly because she does not believe in office romances. She does not think that you can have a professional working environment when you are in a personal relationship. Besides, Rosalyn, you are the only woman I am romantically and emotionally involved with, and I want our relationship to grow to the next level. Will you trust me and believe I only want to be with you.

Rosalyn was overtaken by Johnny's silver tongue. He was blessed to be able to talk himself in or out of anything he wanted. Rosalyn might have been in love, but she is not dumb. She knows what she is seeing, rather he wants to admit it or not. Rosalyn turned her back on Johnny and was just about to go out of the office for lunch, when she turned to face him again saying, "Johnny, I can't believe you don't realize that you are in love with Sallie. You need to wake up and realize that before someone gets hurt. I can't have you around my son and you are not serious about me." Johnny said, "Rosalyn, I told you that I only have eyes for you. I love only you. I don't know what I have to do to prove this to you."

Rosalyn knew that it was something that he could do to show her that she was the only one that he loved, and it was to fire Sallie, and let her stay. Rosalyn was a sensible woman. She knew that was not right, nor appropriate, so she did not even voice that evil thought. She left for lunch, and Johnny thought long and hard, on what had transpired between him and Rosalyn, and then between him and Sallie. He finally realized, he was in love with two different women, and he did not know what he was going to do about it.

Rosalyn returned from lunch, and Johnny left to go to lunch after she had came back. He returned in an hour. The end of the day was long and dreary, but it was time for him and Rosalyn to talk about their future, after her job ends. The only thing she had planned was to start on the project of decorating the new apartments she was under a contract with, and take care of her son. Rosalyn knew that she and Johnny had to discuss what their future would be when she no longer worked there. They both decided that they were going to try to go to the next level in their relationship by Johnny spending more time with her son, Greg, Jr.

The middle of the next week came, Sallie resumed her office duties. Sallie and Johnny appeared to have more than just an office relationship. They were even closer friends than they were before she left on a leave of absence. Their relationship was different then he and Linda's relationship. Linda and Johnny acted like sisters and brothers, but Johnny and Sallie shared a strong enduring relationship that surpassed a physical attraction. Their relationship was more like two souls joining together in blissful joy. As if the two of them belonged together. The two of them denied it because they were both involved in other relationships that were also as enduring as theirs appeared to be. When Johnny, Linda, and Sallie were together, Linda teased them how they were with each other, but they never would act on their feelings because they respected each other, and did not want to cause problems with the other people they were involved with.

Chapter Eleven

Linda returned to work, and Johnny and her, resumed their daily lunch visits at Easy Meal diner. He loved Linda so much. She was so easy to talk to. When Friday came, Johnny and Sallie worked as usual. The scheduled traveling date for him to go to Orlando, Florida was postponed for three weeks. Sallie and Johnny decided to go on break.

They began to get into a deep conversation about the kind of woman or man they wanted to marry. Johnny said, "Yea, speaking of marriage, when am I going to meet your boyfriend. Linda told me that she met him. By the way, keep your sister away from your boyfriend. She goes on and on how gorgeous he is." Sallie said, "Johnny, I know you are not jealous with the beautiful woman that you have." You better be satisfied, and go on with your life. Besides, you are practically a dad, and have an already made family."

Johnny said, "Yea, that's right. Rosalyn and her son are great. We all get along very well. Greg, Jr. and I clicked the first time we met, but I can't help but to feel like there is something missing." He looked at Sallies beautiful eyes in the most enduring way, and said, "Sallie have you ever been in a great relationship, but at times, you feel like, maybe you have stronger feelings for someone else?"

Sallie jokingly said, "No, not lately. What are you talking about? You know that you are in love with my sister, Linda." Johnny said, "Sallie, I'm serious. I sometimes wonder is this it? Is this the woman that I am to spend the rest of my life with? I know she is great, and her son is wonderful, but Sallie when I look at you, when I talk to you, it is like there is no one else in the room but you and I. Even if there is a room full of people, I feel like you and I are the only two people on earth."

As he took her hand he pulled her close to his body and whispered in her ear, Sallie I know you feel it to. It is time for us to admit it." Sallie could feel the heat rising in her body. She was already quite aware of Johnny's ability to talk a stubborn donkey into obeying him, sort of speak, but she allowed him to continue. She could hear the passion in his voice every time he spoke a word to her. She could feel the warmth of his breath as his lips caressed her lips, and he very lovingly kissed her, as they both melted in each other arms. Things became very hot instantly.

Johnny began to whisper in Sallie's ears and say, "Sallie, I desperately need to show you how much, I am richly drawn to you. This feeling overcomes me, more and more, every moment we spend with each other. Sallie I.........." Before Johnny could finish his sentence, Sally contained herself and pulled away from him. This was the hardest thing she had ever had to do. The temptation to give into Johnny was so strong that she almost gave in to the sinful pleasure.

Johnny looked at her with wanting in his eyes as he asked her very softly, "Why did you pull away?" Why want you let me show you how much I really care about you? Sally, I believe I am falling in l..............." Sally put her finger to Johnny's lips before he finished his declaration of his heart felt feelings he had for her.

She ran out of the office and began to cry in the unisex bathroom down the hall. She felt like her whole world was beginning to crumble, and the weight of the world was upon her shoulders. Sallie knew that she almost gave into temptation, and that was something she did not practice doing. She knew that Johnny was not alone in feeling the way that he was feeling toward her. She also had those same feelings. She just did not know how to handle it. She was in unfamiliar territory. She had never been in a love triangle before. She felt so ashamed of herself.

Johnny finally was able to locate her in the unisex bathroom down the hallway. He went into the bathroom and approached her very slowly because he did not want her to run away from him again. He placed his lean muscular arms around her, and comforted her until she felt safe, and began to calm down, and stop crying. He began to warmly talk to Sallie by asking her, "Sallie, why are you running away from me? Why want you let me show and tell you how deeply, I feel for you? I feel strongly, you are that woman I have been praying, searching for, and missing in my life. I know that you are my soul mate and that we belong together. We have denied our love for too long, and I know if you are honest with yourself, you feel the same way too. Sallie what are you so afraid of?"

Sallie looked at Johnny with tears in her eyes, as she spoke in a whimpering voice, "Johnny you belong to someone else and I do too. I feel like I have betrayed the Lord and my faith, not to mention my boyfriend, Jeffery, by almost giving into you in the office. Johnny, I pulled away from you because I don't want to get hurt. You are already in a committed relationship. I have seen you with Rosalyn. I hear you when you say how well you get along with her son, Greg, Jr. You both seem so complete. I personally don't want to come between something that appears to be so solid.

Johnny was taken back to reality at those words. He knew that if Rosalyn ever found out about what just happened between him and Sallie, she would be utterly destroyed. Not to mention, her son, Greg, Jr. The three of them had bonded so closely that he knew he had to start thinking about the other people he was involved with. He did not want anyone to get hurt, even though, he had came to the realization that Sallie was truly his soul mate.

Johnny apologized and backed off of Sallie from that point on, and they both began to express only a professional relationship while at work. When they were at home and around Linda, it was hard for them to hide their actual feelings, but they were determined to work hard at not hurting the other the people that were in their lives. Linda could feel the tension every time they were in the midst of each other. Rosalyn and Johnny continued their relationship, but Johnny could not deny his feelings for Sallie, any longer. His feelings for her were growing stronger and stronger each day even though they both tried to stop seeing each other so much outside of work.

Chapter Twelve

Rosalyn and her son, Greg, Jr., began to spend a lot of time with Greg, Sr. It appeared that Rosalyn and Greg, Sr. were rekindling their former close relationship. The three of them started doing more things as a family, trying to please their son, but at the same time their feelings for each other were growing to a heating desire. Although, Johnny and Rosalyn were pursuing their relationship, it was obvious that Rosalyn and Greg Sr. were rekindling their love toward one another.

One Sunday warm evening, after Rosalyn, Greg Sr., and Greg, Jr. had spent a wonderful day at the park. Rosalyn and Greg, Sr. put their son to bed. He actually had fallen asleep in the car before they made it home because he had played so hard at the park. Greg. Sr. was a 6'3 lean muscular 34years old man with blonde wavy hair. He had brown hazel eyes that had a little spark of blue in them. He had perfect bone structure as if he was from an Indian descent, but his skin tone was fair. He was definitely a handsome man to look at. Their son looked just like him, except for the fact his hair was sandy and his skin tone was darker because of Rosalyn having a darker skin tone.

Greg, Sr. walked over to the CD player and put in a song that he knew, both of them enjoyed. It just happened to be from the collection of his all time favorite group, Boys to Men. The song was called, "I'll make love to you, like you want me too." Rosalyn did not think anything about his song selection because she loved the song so much.

Greg, Sr. walked smoothly, yet very sure of himself, over to Rosalyn, and asked Rosalyn to dance with him.

Rosalyn almost said no because she knew that once Greg, Sr. had her in his arms and close to his body, it was all over. Greg, Sr. was so smoking hot and sexy that he was so hard for any woman to resist him. Especially, since he knew how to work his body to his advantage, so that a woman would melt in his arms when he slowed danced with her. He would give her a total indication how he performed in bed, when he danced with her. The only thing that was different from the dancing was that he was ten times better in the actual sexual act.

Rosalyn tried to break a loose from his embrace, but she was mesmerized by his beautiful eyes. That was always her weakness concerning him. His eyes made her feel as if, at any given moment, he could say anything he wanted to do to her, and she would say, "Yes, yes, yes, I will do anything you say." Greg, Sr. seductively put his arms around her tiny waist and pulled her closer to his hips. She was barely to his chest, but somehow they were perfectly adjoined at the hips. He began to move his hips in a smooth side to side motion as he held her intimately. They moved slowly across the floor lost in each other arms. Greg, Sr. learned how to dance very seductively when he was doing a movie in Mexico.

He was a famous actor that also has a doctorate degree in Physical Therapy. He was spotted by a casting director when he was working part time at a diner in San Francisco, Ca. The casting director talked him into auditioning for a small part in a romantic comedy. As a result of him doing so well in that movie, and his presence was such a hit with women. He instantly became a well sought after, leading man that every director wanted to cast.

However, due to him being away so much, and Greg, Jr. not having a chance to see his dad that often, Rosalyn decided to go on with her life, and raise her son by herself. She was already practically doing that anyway. If it was not for her two brothers and her parents, she really did not know what she was going to do, or how she was going to finish school. She was very grateful to her family for being there for her when she needed them the most. Prior to Greg, Sr. becoming an actor, he worked at the Memorial Hospital as a Physical Therapist Sr. Director.

He started working part time at the diner to make a little extra money because he and Rosalyn had just found out that they were expecting a baby. He knew that the job at the diner was temporary, but he wanted to put enough money back for a trust fund for their son, and help Rosalyn to take more classes to finish her degree, due to their baby was going to be born in the next seven months. He wanted Rosalyn to take it easy, but she was determined to finish college before she had their child, even if she had to take online classes that were very expensive along with her day classes at the University. Rosalyn was able to finish her senior year before she had Greg, Jr., but times were hard at first because Greg, Sr. was always out on location shooting a film.

Greg, Sr. tried to keep in touch with them and come home as often as he could, but he was always too busy. His classic great looks kept him having leading roles. Greg Sr. knew that he had lost his family because of his career. He took some time off from acting, so that he could recapture the love that he and Rosalyn once shared because he wanted his family back. He loved his family. He thought he was working hard to provide for his family, but the reverse occurred, he lost his family because he worked so much.

Greg Sr. began to move more seductively as they danced. The song, I'll make love to you like you want me too, began to make their bodies steaming hot with burning pleasure, as they both became lost in the moment. Rosalyn met Greg, Sr. movements as they danced. Greg, Sr. carefully dipped Rosalyn backward. He leaned toward her, and his sweet, perfectly, moistened lips touched her perfectly, soft, smooth lips that were warm with wanting pleasure. They embraced in a long steamy kiss as Greg, Sr. skillfully slow danced them right into Rosalyn's bed.

Greg, Sr., in one gesture, unzipped the one piece, red dress, off of her little perfectly fit body. He was somehow able to continue to passionately kiss her, while undressing them both. They started out slow and passionate until the movement of their bodies became an explosion of exotic fast paced, rhythmic pleasure. All of the love, hurt, pain, good times, and bad times, they had shared, was acted out in their passionate love making that drove them into a heated frenzy. They both climaxed with so much pleasure, that afterwards they both fell asleep until the next morning. They both made sure they were up and dressed before Greg, Jr. woke up because they did not want to confuse him. They did not quite understand what was going on, much more, to explain it to a four year old child.

Rosalyn, Greg Sr., and Greg, Jr. spent the whole Monday with each other. There was no doubt that the three of them were finding their way back to each other. At the end of the day before Greg, Sr. left to go home, he and Rosalyn discussed where they would go from here. After last night and the fact they were spending so much time together as a family, was conflicting Rosalyn thoughts about her and Johnny's relationship. Rosalyn and Greg, Sr. decided to decrease the amount of time they were spending together and not to engage in any more sexual encounters while she was in a relationship with someone else. Greg, Sr. agreed, but he was not about to give in so easily. Not after the wonderful weekend they had shared together as a family. He wanted his family back, and he was going to do all he could to get them back.

CHAPTER THIRTEEN

THE NEXT MORNING, Rosalyn decide to stop by the office to see Johnny because she felt guilty over the things that happened between her and Greg, Sr. On her way to Johnny's job, she dropped Greg, Jr. off at school and picked up Johnny some breakfast. Rosalyn walked in on Sallie and Johnny laughing and talking about one of their case conference meeting with their senior boss that was telling corny jokes and thought that they were funny. Rosalyn did not know that they were talking about their boss corny jokes.

When Rosalyn walked into their office, she noticed that they seemed professional enough, but she could tell that something was causing a lot of tension between the two of them. Little did she know that the tension was caused by their pinned up passion for one another. They promised each other that they would not act on their passion for each other because they were involved with other people.

As Rosalyn walked into the office approaching, Sallie's desk, both Sallie and Johnny tried not to act like the two of them were the only people in the room, as they were often accused of doing. Even though, Rosalyn could look through their act, she did not like it all, but she kept her cool. Almost simultaneously, both Johnny and Sallie said, "Hello Rosalyn. How are you? It is so good to see you. Come in. Have a seat."

Johnny walked over to Rosalyn and kissed her softly on the lips, and said, "Hi baby. Is everything okay?" Rosalyn said, "Hello", to Sallie and then said to Johnny, "Oh, I am fine. I just wanted to stop by and say hello. I have not seen you in a couple of days. What have you been up to?" Johnny said to Sallie, "Excuse us, Sallie."

He began to talk softly to Rosalyn asking her to come into his office. He said to her, "Have a seat, sweetheart. I have been hanging out at home not doing much of anything. I knew that you and Greg. Jr. was hanging out with Greg, Sr. I came by Sunday evening, and saw that Greg, Sr.'s car was still at your apartment. I got out of the car and was about to knock on the door, but I did not want to destroy Greg, Jr. chance in spending time with both of his parents. He is a very respectable little boy. He deserves to spend time with both his parents every now and then, but I admit I was a little jealous because I wanted to spend that quality time with the two of you.

Rosalyn nervously said, "Oh you came by the house Sunday evening? About what time, did you stop by? She was questioning Johnny because she knew the passionate love making her and Greg. Sr. was involved in Sunday, evening, and hoped that Johnny had not witnessed any of it. Johnny said, "Oh, I came by about 6:00 pm. I saw that you and Greg, Sr. were talking seriously about something. I did not want to interrupt, so I left." Rosalyn was relieved. She knew that she and Greg Sr. did not start engaging in what they experienced, until after they had talked about what fun the three of them had at the park that day. Rosalyn said to Johnny, "Ok good. Greg, Sr. and I were talking about the things they had experienced at the park. Thank you for that time, but you could have made your presence known. After all, you are my boyfriend."

Johnny replied, "That is quite alright. What are you doing tonight? I would like to take you and Greg, Jr. to dinner tonight." Rosalyn said, "I'm sorry Johnny, but Greg, Sr. told Greg, Jr. that he wanted him to come over his house for dinner. He asked me to come as well. I hope you don't mind."

Johnny said feeling a little left out, "Ok sure. Maybe we can get together this weekend before I leave to go to Orlando, Florida. Rosalyn said, "Sure, I will make plans for us to be together this weekend. Do you want to go to lunch with me? It is almost 12:00 noon. I know I brought you breakfast, but it is cold now. I want to take you out for lunch. Johnny said, "Yes, I would love to go to lunch with my beautiful girlfriend.

As he and Rosalyn was walking out of his office, he told Sallie that he was going out for lunch and that he would be back in an hour. As Johnny and Rosalyn walked out of the office, Sallie tried her best not to be jealous of Johnny and Rosalyn relationship. Although, she wished it was her going out to lunch with Johnny instead of Rosalyn, she was still set against having an office romance. She resisted the temptation of giving into it.

The Lord knows she had many opportunities to do so. Johnny and Rosalyn went to a nearby café down the street and not to his usual eating place at the Easy Meal diner. Johnny and Rosalyn had a great lunch and he made it back to work within an hour just as he promised. They kissed each other passionately and said goodbye as Rosalyn dropped him back at the office. Rosalyn picked up Greg, Jr. from school and the two of them spent a quiet evening together watching TV and Rosalyn helping Greg, Jr. doing his homework. Afterwards, they both fell fast asleep.

Johnny's days of going out and hanging out until late hours were all over. Johnny was officially going out with one woman exclusively. Johnny decided to go over Linda's after work. He and Linda had a great evening together laughing and talking. Linda relentlessly teased Johnny for falling in love with her sister, Sallie, and hopelessly continuing a relationship with Rosalyn because he did not want to hurt Rosalyn or her son Greg, Jr.

Johnny of course denied his feeling of being hopelessly in love with Sallie even though he knew that she was telling truth. He was so frustrated because Sallie would not let him show her just how much he really loved her, not to mention just telling her that he did. Johnny did mention to Linda that he was concerned that Rosalyn, Greg, Sr. and Greg, Jr. was spending a lot of time together as a family, and that he felt left out. Linda told him that she knew it did not feel very good at this time, but that he should let everything play itself out. In the end it will be best for all.

She did warn Johnny that he and Rosalyn needed to re-evaluate their relationship to see if they were still on the same page. Although

Johnny tried desperately not to reveal to Linda just how deeply he was in love with her sister, Sallie, he could not deny the fact that Rosalyn was drawing closer to her ex- husband Greg, Sr. Johnny also knew that within the next week he was going to have to go to Orlando, Florida to conduct the final business on the Penn Hotel.

He knew that he was going to be out there for two to three months. He had already asked Sallie to accompany him on that business trip to help him keep his paper work in order. She had already told him that she would. After all, she was his personal assistant. Sallie was tempted to say no because she did not know how Rosalyn would feel about it. She asked Johnny to make sure he discussed it with her so that everything would be in the open. The rest of the week went on smoothly.

Saturday morning, Johnny called Rosalyn, and asked her to come by his house that afternoon. Johnny knew that it was Greg, Sr. weekend to have Greg, Jr. Rosalyn showed up about 1:00 pm. They had lunch together. Johnny had cooked a meatloaf, homemade mashed potatoes with chives, and sweet corn. He had chilled some sparkling grape juice because he or Rosalyn drank alcohol. He had baked some French bread to eat with his meal.

Johnny and his brother learned how to cook from both of their parents. They used cooking as a means of family fellowship. After they had eaten lunch, they relaxed on the couch in the den. Johnny began to remind Rosalyn that on Monday he was scheduled to be in Orlando, Florida to put the finishing touches on the Penn Hotel Suite chains, and that his personal assistant, Sallie would be accompanying him.

Rosalyn felt very sad to find out that the week had finally came that Johnny would be scheduled to be out of town, and she did not like the ideal that Sallie was going with him because she knew how close they were. Rosalyn also was concerned about what was rekindling between her and Greg, Sr. was altogether too real to deny. Rosalyn decided not to play into her fears, and just relax in the moment of being close to her boyfriend in the way that made both of them feel very relaxing. They made love and held each other all night long. On Sunday morning both of them said their goodbyes and Rosalyn left to go pick up Greg, Jr. from over his dad's house.

Chapter Fourteen

The weekend passed quickly, and Monday had come. Johnny and Sallie arrived at the airport and hour before their scheduled departure. The project was long and time consuming. The paperwork was hideous. He was so happy that Sallie had accompanied him because she was doing a good job of keeping the paperwork in an organized manner. Sallie and Johnny could not help but to draw closer to each other emotionally even though they were not having a physical relationship.

Rosalyn tried to keep in contact with Johnny while he was in Orlando, but it became increasingly harder, day by day. Rosalyn and Greg, Sr. could not help but to rekindle their past love. There love was definitely resurfacing and they both were quite aware of it. Even Greg, Jr. was aware of it. It was hard for them to hide it. They had been caught up in the moment making hot passionate love with each other at least twice since Johnny had left.

It had become increasingly clear that it was hard for them to stay apart from one another. Greg, Sr. had on a number of occasions expressed his love toward Rosalyn in words, action, and emotionally. One thing Greg, Sr. was very successful in doing was expressing his views, ideas, and love. That was the very thing that attracted Rosalyn to Greg, Sr. because of his great ability to do this. The distance of Greg, Sr. being away grew them apart as a couple, but now he was back to reclaim his family, and he was not going to stop until he did.

Greg, Sr. asked Rosalyn to become his wife again and he promised her that it would be much better this time. He convincingly, let her know that he knew the reason why their marriage did not survive. The main reason was because he put his job first. He thought he was doing the right thing by taking all those acting roles to provide for his family, but he did not know he was actually losing his family until he received the divorce papers.

He told Rosalyn that he really did not understand why she sent the divorce papers, but the adjoining letter she had attached to it made him realize how hurt she was, and he could not help but to feel her pain, and that was the only reason why he signed the divorce papers without a fight. He told her that he was doing all he could to regain her trust and win back his family because he loved them so much.The three of them continued to spend a lot of time together.

They even joined a local church and began to get counseling by the pastor of that church. The pastor helped them to see that even though they were rekindling their love for one another, they were not being a very good example to their son. It was brought up by Rosalyn that she was also involved with another man that she had introduced to Greg, Jr. and the both of them had bonded very well.

She was afraid that she was sending Greg, Jr. mixed messages, and she was ashamed of her actions. Pastor Walker had helped her to see what she was experiencing was not uncommon when we act out our fleshly nature, but when we come into the knowledge that we are doing something wrong, then that is when it becomes a challenge for us to do what is right.

He let them know that in the scriptures, Roman 3:23, states "For all have sinned and come short of the glory of God." He also let them know that according to St. John 1:9 states, "If we confess of our sins then he is faithful and just to forgive us and cleanse us from all unrighteousness." He went on to encourage them to put God and their child first and be a good example so that he can learn to do the right things. He also encouraged them both to think about their lives and the people that are intertwined in their inner circle. He prayed that the two of them would make God the head of their lives and ask him to order their steps to bring about his perfect plan for their lives.

Several weeks had passed, Rosalyn and Greg, Sr. had agreed to stop sleeping with one another and to put space between the two of them, allowing her enough time to find out which man she wanted to have a future with so that she would not continue to send their son conflicting messages in which man she was in love with. The sad thing was that she had noticed that her body was changing. She began to get sick and nauseated. She had noticed that she had gone a month without having her monthly menstrual cycle.

She had made her mind to go to her Gynecologist to get a blood pregnancy test done. Her doctor sent her to the lab and she was told that she would get the results within a couple of days. She had the lab test done and Wednesday the results were in. She received notification via mail to come in to see her Gynecologist to receive her results. Her fears were confirmed. She was pregnant. It was also confirmed that she was one month pregnant. They did a HCG titer. She was not surprised who the father was because Johnny had already been gone seven weeks I Orlando, Florida, and the way her and Greg, Sr. was going at it, she knew that if she played with fire she eventually was going to get burnt.

The dilemma was not that she was pregnant but how she was going to tell the two men that she was in a relationship with. She knew that Greg. Sr. would be overjoyed, and he would finally want to put the final touches of reclaiming his family by proposing to her again. She also knew that it was going to be hard for her to tell Johnny. She pondered for weeks on how she would tell them that she was pregnant.

Chapter Fifteen

In the meantime, Johnny had finally been given the chance to confess his undying love for Sallie. He had told her that even if she wanted to continue to deny her true feeling of being passionately in love with him, he was not going to deny himself from expressing his enduring heartfelt love for her. He realized that the love they shared was strange because they had not been together physically, but they had such an emotional bond that was closer than any physical relationship could ever be. Adding the physical element to the equation could only make things more pleasurable and enduring.

Their love was definitely not ordinary. It was unusual. It was much different from his relationship with Rosalyn. Although he and Rosalyn shared a loving relationship, it was nothing to be compared to what he had with Sallie. What he had with Sallie was like a breath of fresh air. Something that felt true and everlasting. Their relationship was like being in the presence of your soul mate. It was a match made in Heaven. One that the scriptures talk about, "If God put you together let no man put you asunder. It is an unbreakable bond.

Knowing all these things, Johnny was no longer going to abide by the promise he made to Sallie about keeping their feelings pinned up and not acting on them. One Friday evening after he had taken her to a nice romantic Japanese restaurant, he looked into her shiny beautiful eyes and spoke strongly but sweetly to her as he grabbed her hand in between his two hands, "Sallie I can no longer pretend that I don't love you. I have loved you every since I found out what kind of woman you truly are. I love your independence, your belief in God, your integrity, your love for your family, your humble spirit, and your ability to make even the meanest person smile and be nice.

Sallie I can truthfully say that all these attributes that you possess makes you the most desirable woman that I have ever known. When I am with you, I never feel alone. It is as if we are the only two people in the world. You are my lifeline, the other half of my soul. I love you like Christ loved the church. I will promise to give you all of me. I will promise to take care of you. I will promise to be your protector, and next to God, I will promise to love you forever."

Sallie allowed Johnny to speak his heart without interruption. She knew that it was going to happen sooner a later. Johnny kneeled down on his knees and pulled a beautiful mid size shiny diamond ring out and said these most spell bounding words, "Sweetheart, I know you know that I love you, and I know that you love me. I want to spend the rest of my life with you the right way. Will you marry me and be my wife for all eternity as long as we both shall leave?"

Sallie was so amazed that Johnny was speaking such heartfelt words to her that she was moved to tears. She was almost ready to run out of the restaurant, but before she could something froze her in place and commanded her to answer him. Sallie turned and looked at the sincerity in Johnny's face as he knelt down before her with the beautiful ring in his hand. She knew that over the last two months that they had became so close that it was hard for her not to have fallen in love with him. Besides being the most handsome man she had ever known, she knew that what Johnny was telling her was true.

She knew that Johnny was a good man, and she found out that he was also a believer. She felt like Johnny always wanted to settle down with a good woman. He was just going to the wrong places trying to find her. The relationship between Jeffery and her did not work out either because he did not think their relationship could last during the three months she was to be in Orlando, Florida. They agreed to break up and just be friends.

She leaned toward Johnny's face and kissed him on his lips and said, "Johnny you are an amazing man. I truly am blessed that such a good man would want to settle down his wild oaks for me. I must admit, that I have loved you ever since I got to know you better when my sister Linda broke her leg in the car wreck she had. Seeing that you have been such a loving friend toward my little sister showed me what a stand up guy you were. Johnny, I love you too. I too believe we were made for each other. I know that it must be destiny that we come together as one because I was ready to run out of this restaurant, away from you and your love, because I was scared that I was going to be hurt. Johnny, something stopped me and commanded me to give you an answer. I believe it was the Lord. I know, now, that the love you have for me supersedes any love you could have for any other woman.

Sallie continued to let Johnny know that her feelings for him are very strong, and at times, she has to wrestle with her flesh, not to give in to being with him intimately, all day, and all night. She said, "You see Johnny, I have been praying to God for a long time for him to send me a God fearing man that would love me like Christ loved the church and be concerned about my well being. This man would love me with all of his heart and not be ashamed to call me his wife or show public affection toward me."

Johnny continued to patiently listen to Sallie as she shared her feelings, "You see Johnny, all along, I knew you were the type of man I was looking for, but it seemed like you were looking for love in all the wrong places. You devoted your time to the clubs and did not depend on the Lord to send you the type of woman that was more than just a physically attraction. If you remember, I used to tell you all the time, "Johnny, I am praying for you." I knew you were better than what you were settling for."

Johnny looked at Sallie with a love so sincere that anybody in their presence could notice how much he loved her. Sallie continues to pour out her heart to Johnny. "You see I never forgot how you told me you were a believer and you wanted to settle down with a good woman, but just saying mere words are not good enough. You have to put your beliefs in action. I saw you changing with Rosalyn in a good way. That is why I did not want to interfere with what you two had together."

Johnny and Sallie moved to a bench in the area in which they were in to relax as Sallie continued to pour her heart out to Johnny. "I was confused because I had started to be drawn to you and I did not know why. I knew that you wanted to get to know me better, but I was afraid of getting hurt because you belonged to someone else. I am the type of woman if I give myself to you. You have my whole body, heart, and soul."

Sallie looked into Johnny's beautiful eyes as she continues to speak earnestly to him, "I don't play around and I was not about to settle on a man that did not want to recognize a good woman that had high integrity standards. I guess, I was afraid that you would be with me for a little while, and then drop me to be with another woman. That was not going to work for me.

I wanted someone that knew what they wanted and was not going to be torn between two women. Johnny, I want to be with you sexually, emotionally, and spiritually, but I cannot successfully do any of these things until you make up your mind on which woman you want to be with. If it is me that you want, and all other ties are cut, then and only then, will I be happy to be you wife and marry you."

Johnny spoke to Sallie very softly and sincerely, "Sallie truthfully, I want to be with you. Whether you believe it or not, your prayers have been answered. I'm ready to settle down and stop chasing women in the clubs. You are right. Since I have graduated from college, I have been partying quite a bit. I have been burning the candle on both ends. Working all day and partying all night."

Johnny continues to speak to Sallie with a sincere tone, " My parents and even my younger brother, Cornelius, who is already married, have been getting on to me for the life style I have chosen to live. They knew that I had fallen far from how I was raised. My parents taught me to respect God's ways, apply them to my lifestyle choices, and to respect women. My father was a big advocate for both. He was a prime example to my brother and our little sister, and myself, how to respect God. He would pray with us every night before we went to sleep. He and my mom raised us in church. It is funny, my entire family was very active in church, and still are, all of them but me. I am now trying to get back into church."

Sallie looked intently into Johnny's eyes as he spoke to her. She thought about running away, but it was something holding her from doing it. Johnny continued, "But I am the Prodigal son that has strayed away from the teachings of our parents. I am not attending weekly worship services nor am I reading my bible everyday to help me be strong in the Lord and in the power of his might. That is possibly the reason why I am so drawn to you and your sister. You two exemplify what I want in a woman and the type of woman that fits the way my sister, brother and I were raised.

You are also right when you stated that I have been looking for love in all the wrong places. I became accustomed to those types of women when I was in college. I pursued this type because I was not ready to settle down. However, you don't know this, but I was also praying for the type of woman that I was compatible with. In addition, she would also help me to get back to my roots in the Lord."

Johnny stood up from the bench and walked closer to Sallie as he reached out and grabbed her hand helping her to stand on her feet as he spoke softly, "You two remind me of my mother in the way that you both are Christian women, full of integrity, devoted, loving, and amazingly beautiful. You two possess qualities that not many women possess. I have seen it in several women along my life, including my mother and sister. Even my little sister, Rochelle, is engaged to marry a young man that she has been dating for eight years. This man waited on my sister until she graduated from law school and began to work at my father's law firm, "Lambert and Lamberts."

Johnny continued to choose his words carefully as he spoke to Sallie, "Both of my siblings and I followed my father's footsteps, and we became a family of lawyers. Sallie as far as Rosalyn and I are concern, I want to be truthful with you. I do love Rosalyn. She is a great woman and mother, but I believe she and Greg, Sr. are finding their way back to each other. The main reason why they divorced was because Greg, Sr. became a famous actor, and was away from home almost all the time shooting films. Greg, Sr. did not realize that his work habits were driving his family apart. Rosalyn refused to remain in a long distance relationship with a man that her son would not know as his father because he was always gone, no matter how much she loved him."

Johnny carefully selected his tone of voice because he did not want Sallie to run away from him. He continued to talk honestly to Sallie. "Sallie, I need you to know that my feelings for you are much more serious and in depth than my relationship with Rosalyn. I am not trying to compare the two of you because you both are high on my list of as respectable beautiful women. But it is something about the connection that is between you and I that shuts the entire world down around us. It seems as if you and I are the only two people on the planet when we are in each other's company. I don't mean to talk in riddles, but it is something beautiful going on between the two of us that is very hard to deny or resist. It is like we were made for each other, and we are supposed to be with each other in order to be complete. It sounds strange, but I really believe this is true. Our bond grows each time we are in each others' company.

Sallie agreed. She continued to inform Johnny of the fact she knew that it was God answering her prayers by sending her the type of man that she had been sincerely praying for all of these years. On this hope, she was able to keep her body pure from having a sexual relationship with a man. Although along the years, she was greatly tempted and tested. She was now thirty years old and was ready be married and have a family. She wanted her mom not to be too old to enjoy her grandchildren.

Although, her mom was very active, she was 54 years old, and she always wanted grand children. Sallie was her only child, and even though Linda was not her biological daughter, she loved her as if she was. Linda was able to spend some time with Sallie and her mom during the summers, but because they lived in two different states, it was difficult for them to see each other as much as they wanted to.

Linda was raised by her mom's sister and husband who had three other children. They raised Linda in a loving Christian home just like Sallie's mom raised her. Sallie had a wonderful step father that helped raised her to be a strong woman. He taught her how to resist men that was just after her body and not her soul. Fortunately, he taught her very well. By the help of the Lord, and her step father, she was able to dodge a lot of mishaps that could have resulted in a teenage pregnancy. Sallie's beauty and strength made her very desirable. She attracted a lot of male attention that started in her preteen years.

Sallie was very involved with her father and stepmother before their tragic death due to a serious car accident. That is how she and Linda became so close. Their families lived in the same town. Although Sallie's mother and her dad got a divorce, they still remained great friends. Their friendship enabled Sallie and Linda to be raised together, even though they officially lived in separate households. There was a great understanding between the two adult couples when it came to Sallie and Linda. They did not want to break the bond between the two girls. Johnny was relieved that Sallie felt comfortable enough with him to tell him about her family. He invited her to continue their conversation at a cozy restaurant in Orlando. They decided to a Japanese restaurant

Sallie enjoyed getting to know Johnny better that night at the Japanese restaurant. They both let go of some of the reserves that held them back from sharing their true feelings for each other. They both realized before they started a physical relationship they needed to get to know each other to see if they were compatible.

Johnny and Sallie finished the project of the Penn Hotel chain and was able to enjoy some of the fun spots their last week in Orlando, Florida. The two of them even had a chance to go to Disney World. They had a blast. Orlando, Florida was truly a beautiful warm city that had a lot of places to hang out and have some nice clean fun. Sallie did not go out to clubs, but they found other place to go like sea world, museums, art shows, and the various surrounding restaurants to occupy the rest of their time there. The end of the week came fast and they were now headed back home to Phoenix, Arizona. The two of them were successful in not only completing the Penn Hotel project but also in drawing closer to one another.

Chapter Sixteen

When they made it home, they rested. Of course Sallie told Linda about how much she had learned about Johnny. She told Linda how Johnny had a strong background in the Lord, but he strayed away from the teachings his parents taught him, his brother, and his sister during and after his college years. Sallie also told Linda that Johnny's family lived in San Antonio, Texas and they are a family of lawyers.

His brother and sister work with their father at the Lambert and Lamberts law firm. Johnny informed me that he was more like the Prodigal son that moved away from his family, and did not fall into the family traditions of working at the family law firm. He was looking for a woman that was strong in her beliefs, devoted, loving, that would help him get back to his roots. He was now ready to settle down. He explained to me that he does love Rosalyn, and he believes Rosalyn is a great woman and mother, but deep down inside, he believes that she and Greg, Sr. are finding their way back to each other.

Sallie informed Linda that Rosalyn had told Johnny earlier on in their relationship what led to her divorce to Greg, Sr. who is a famous actor. Rosalyn divorced Greg Sr. because he was always away from home shooting films. As a result, they grew apart because Rosalyn refused to carry on a long distance relationship with a man that her son would hardly know was his father.

However, Johnny believes that Greg, Sr. has taken time off from his acting career to reclaim his family. He has been so devoted to spending time with Greg, Jr. and tries his best to spend quality time with the three of them. Sallie told Linda that Johnny also believes that he has succeeded in winning her back. He had rarely spoken to her while they were in Orlando, Florida even though he tried to call her often to check on her and Greg, Jr.

Linda was overjoyed on the news of Johnny and Sallie finally breaking through their fears and realizing how much they were truly destined to be with each other. The two of them were the only ones denying this because everybody else that witnessed them together knew this all along, even Rosalyn. This is why Rosalyn feared them two going to Orlando, Florida together. She had confessed this to Linda while Johnny and Sallie were away.

Over the next two weeks, Johnny, Mr. Lincoln, Sallie and the other contractors were together two finish the project of the apartment complexes in the center area of Phoenix, Arizona. The apartments were beautiful. On June the 5th of the next year, they would be ready for the grand opening and start accepting applications from desiring residents. Johnny had tried multiple times over the last three weeks to contact Rosalyn, but she has never returned his call.

Meanwhile, Rosalyn thought about Johnny often. She had heard that Johnny and Sallie were back home by some of her office friends she had made while working with Johnny. She wanted to call Johnny back, but did not know how to tell him that her and Greg, Sr. had renewed their relationship, vows, and were expecting another child. Rosalyn had accepted Greg, Sr.'s proposal of marriage because she wanted her children to know their dad.

She also knew that she had falling back in love with him, and he truly was the man that was for her. After thinking long and hard on which man she would choose, she decided to put her son first. She felt that she and Greg, Sr. acted irresponsibly in coming together sexually without regard for anyone else. She knew that Greg, Sr. was a loving man and he sincerely wanted his family back. Rosalyn wanted to tell Johnny that she and Greg Sr. had reunited, but did not know how.

She realized that she reunited with Greg, Sr. because of her premature behavior that ended their relationship and that he was the right man for her.

She knew that she had to let Johnny know, pretty soon, because she was already four months pregnant and she was starting to show. She was one of those women who were blessed in not becoming very large while pregnant, but her child's size would always be within normal range. On another note, she had finished her project of decorating the apartment complexes that she had contracted with, and she was invited to take part in the celebration of the grand opening.

The apartments were very classy, affordable, and had the latest appliances and furniture. They already had a lot of pre-approved applications to start off with. Over the next five months business was as usual the apartment complexes were ready for the grand opening and Johnny had yet to hear from Rosalyn. He felt in his heart that it was because she and Greg Sr. had reunited as a couple. So he never tried to get in contact with her. Besides, he did not know how to let her know that his feelings for Sallie were true and enduring.

Chapter Seventeen

On the evening of June 5th of the next year, all of the people that were involved in making the apartment complexes in the center of Phoenix, Arizona a success were at the Grand opening. Sallie invited Linda to go along with her. Johnny was there. Mr. Lincoln and his wife were also there. All of them were standing at the food bar enjoying each other's company when they noticed a beautiful family coming into the office lounge where they held the grand opening party. The woman was pregnant and strikingly beautiful. As Johnny looked at the woman from afar off, she reminded him of Rosalyn, but he knew that she was not pregnant. As he continued to look at the family, the boy seemed much older than the last time that he had seen Greg, Jr., and he had never met Greg, Sr.

As the family came nearer to the food bar, Johnny and Rosalyn eyes met, and he knew that it was her. He was shocked to see her pregnant. Rosalyn felt ashamed. She had no idea that Johnny or the others would be at the Grand opening party Then she suddenly was reminded to when Johnny was working on an apartment building project in central part of Phoenix, Arizona, that she had told him that she had been selected to do contract work as an interior decorator. She did not know that it was the very project that Johnny was working on.

Johnny did not let her know that he had already set it up with his partners to hire her as the interior decorator for the apartments. They both looked at each other with a bewildered look on their faces, but Rosalyn approached him anyway. She had to because once Greg, Jr. saw Johnny he ran and jumped into his arms. Greg Jr. and Johnny had bonded so quickly and were crazy about each other. Rosalyn introduced Greg, Sr. to Johnny. Greg, Sr. knew about Sallie and Johnny, but he had never met Johnny personally. Johnny and Greg, Sr. shook each other's hands, and voiced that finally they both had a chance to meet, after all, they had heard about the other.

It was very awkward for both Rosalyn and Johnny but they played it off very well. Rosalyn had put herself in such a predicament that she could hardly hide her body language and facial expressions that showed her nervousness. Sallie and Linda looked at each other in amazement of what they saw. They also enjoyed the fact that they were in the same room with Greg, Sr. because he was a famous leading man that all women were crazy about. He was so gorgeous and had supreme acting skills. Rosalyn finally introduced Greg, Sr. and Greg, Jr. to Sallie, Linda, and Mr. Lincoln and his wife.

They managed to engage in some interesting conversations with each other before they mingled with the other guests. As the Grand opening went on, Johnny, Mr. Lincoln, Rosalyn, Sallie, and the others that were involved, received a wonder bonus because of the great work they had done on the apartment complex. Rosalyn received a lot of referrals to decorate other projects from the job she had done for this apartment complex.

The next few days were quiet for Johnny. He thought about how he had seen Rosalyn pregnant and wondered was the child she was carrying his. He decided to call her, but out of respect, he chose not to. It was obvious to him that she and Greg, Sr. had renewed their relationship and love for each other. He did not understand why she was not truthful with him. Even though he knew that he loved Rosalyn, he was in love with Sallie and there was a difference between the two. He could not help but want to bring closure to their relationship. He wanted answers. As he was lying on his den couch, he was in deep thought about these things.

He heard his doorbell ring. He got up to answer the door. It was Rosalyn, she looked disturbed, but it did not take away from her being exceptionally beautiful and very pregnant. She was thirty eight weeks and almost ready for delivery. He let her in. He offered her a seat. Rosalyn declined. She began to speak very softly to him explaining how she felt so ashamed of her actions. She confessed that she should have told him that she and Greg, Sr. were reuniting. She told him about everything. She felt like he deserved to know the truth. He felt very upset to find out that her and Greg, Sr. had slept together multiple times before he and Sallie had gone to Orlando, Florida to finish the Penn Hotel chain project.

She explained that she did not mean to hurt him in this way, but it seemed inevitable that she and Greg, Sr. would reconnect. She told him about the counseling that they had received from their Pastor, and he had told them to stop putting Greg, Jr. in such a compromising position and be examples. She told Johnny that she had confessed to the Pastor that while she was having a sexual relationship with Greg, Sr. she was also having one with him. She felt so guilty that the truth came out. She told Johnny that the Pastor encouraged her to go home and think about her lifestyle choices, and to put her son first in her decision making.

She confessed that she wrestled hard and long between the choice of which man she wanted to build a lifelong relationship with, him or Greg, Sr. She decided in the end that because she ended things prematurely with Greg, Sr. that Greg, Jr. did not get to know his father like he would have if she had not made the decision to divorce Greg, Sr. She realized that her thoughts were totally wrong about Greg, Sr. at the time, and she had not even discussed the divorce with him. She had just explained her feelings on a separate letter, and because Greg, Sr. realized she was in so much pain, he went on and signed the divorce papers, even if he did not want to give up his family. Rosalyn also told him that she felt like he was more in love with Sallie than he was with her, and by them working together and spending so much time with each other, the inevitable was eventually going to happen.

She expressed how she felt that they would be together regardless of the fact they both was in other relationships. She confessed she had always been jealous about how they seemed as if they were the only two people in the world when the two of them were together. Johnny confessed his disappointment of all of this, but also of the fact that he and Sallie truly had a connection to each other that was unexplainable in the beginning, but it became very clear, as they talked and worked together in Orlando, Florida.

Johnny and Rosalyn continued to talk. She told Johnny that the baby she was carrying was, without a doubt, was Greg, Sr.'s because of the time period in which she became pregnant. They had already found out the sex of the baby was a little girl. Johnny was amazed on how frank she was being, now, after all of this. He also realized he wanted the same thing she had with Greg, Sr., with Sallie.

He voiced that he was initially upset about this, but after thinking about Greg, Jr., he figured that it was in his best interest that he be raised by both of his parents like he and his sibling had the blessing to have when they were growing up. He believed in keeping families together, if at all possible. His parents were such great examples of married love. He has always desired to have a good Christian wife, like his mom was to his dad, and the type of mother she was to him, and his siblings. It was very evident in his mind, that the teaching and the upbringing that one has, helps shape the type of person they will become, in one way or the other.

He and Rosalyn were able to regroup and figure things out in order to come to a positive solution. They asked for forgiveness from each other. Although they both realized that it was going to take time before they could actually do that, without having some ill feelings. They still voiced their forgiveness for the other, and vowed to have some type of peaceable friendship for Greg, Jr. sake. Greg, Jr. and Johnny became so close and they did not want to completely remove Johnny out of his life, just because they were no longer a couple.

Rosalyn and Johnny apologized to each other again as she left and vowed to remain friends for Greg Jr. sake. He thought to himself how he appreciated the fact that Rosalyn was woman enough to come over and tell him the whole truth on what had happened and what was now going on. Although he still had mixed feelings about her, he was determined to make Sallie his wife. He was determined not to waste anymore time in doing things her way. He was determined in making their relationship official. He slept on those thoughts and had a very restless night.

Chapter Eighteen

The next morning, he got up and went to church with Sallie and Linda like he had promised, and he spent the rest of the day with them. Linda confessed to them that she had met a wonderful man at her job that often came into the diner to talk with her. She had finally agreed to go out with him. She also confessed that while they were in Orlando, Florida, she got to know him rather well. Linda had invited her boyfriend, Christopher, to come over this evening to finally get a chance to meet them.

At 7:00 pm, Linda's door bell began to ring. Linda went to open the door. It was Christopher. Christopher was a 6ft man that had very strong features. He was long and lean. His body was like the sculpture of a Greek statue. His skin tone was dark and it was not easily apparent on what nationality he was. His hair was black and cut very low. He had a nicely trimmed mustache and beard. He was definitely something to behold.

Sallie could see why Linda was drawn to him. He was not only pleasing to look at, but the sound of his voice was with such power and eloquence that it was mesmerizing. He had a pair of jeans that fit him nicely, with a casual shirt that made him look as if he was ten years younger than he really was. He was actually thirty years old working as a Business Manger of one of the biggest home health companies in

Phoenix, Arizona. Sallie felt that Linda had finally found a man that she could settle down with.

This man was not only successful and childless, but he was also a leader in his church. He also was very devoted to helping other people.

Linda was twenty nine years old this month after her birthday on June eighteenth. She wanted to have children while she was young, so that she could always look as if she was their sister rather than their mother when they became older. But she never found the right man that could hold her heart more than her best friend, Johnny, until she met Christopher. Linda loved children. She and Sallie both did. They loved playing dolls when they were little girls. Johnny had to confess, he liked Christopher to. He seemed like a real cool guy. He was happy for Linda. That made him even more determined to make all of his dreams come true with Sallie.

They all sat down to eat at Linda's dining room table. Christopher had brought some barbecue ribs and all the fixings for four people. Linda had told him that they had not eaten dinner yet. Christopher told her that he would stop to buy some food for everyone. Linda had told him that her sister and their friend, Johnny, were with them. Christopher bought plenty. They ate so much that they didn't want to do anything else but sleep.

Sallie was not having that. She asked everyone to play dominos. They had a good time until Linda and Christopher began to act like they were the only ones in the room. Johnny could see that they wanted to spend a little time together alone, so he asked Sallie if she did not mind walking him home. Sallie also could see her sister and her boyfriend involved in some matters that required the two of them and not two extra people. She said, yes, to Johnny.

Johnny and Sallie walked over to his apartment. He could not help but to stare at her as they walked. By this time, he was so in love with Sallie he could not stand it. It did not do him any good only looking at her, when he knew he wanted to make love to her, over and over again.

Sallie knew that Johnny was staring at her. She tried to play it cool as if he wasn't. Johnny opened the door of his apartment and invited Sallie to have a seat in the living room area. He also asked her if she wanted something to drink. She said, "No." Johnny turned on the TV. He asked her if she wanted to watch a DVD or something. She said, "Yes, what do you have? Johnny said, "I have, "Lets make love tonight", "Adults don't play games", "Endless love", "She is the one", or "Lost in a world wind of love."

Sallie looked at him as if she was telling him with her eyes, "Boy, I know what you are doing." She said, "Stop playing." Johnny said, "I am not playing. These movies are real. You and I act them out every day. Sallie, I am tired of playing." He reached out to her, and pulled her close to him. She could feel his warm breath on her face as he bowed his head to kiss her lips. Sallie, I can't stand it anymore. I love you so much. All I can think about is showing you just how much I love you." Johnny pulled her even closer as he rotated her hips with his, as if he was slow dancing with her without music. He kissed her deeply and pulled her by her hand to his couch. He laid her down and climbed on top of her. He began to kiss her passionately. So much so, that Sallie began to get lost in the heat of the moment.

Johnny began to talk to her in a panting sexually tone. Sallie, I want to make sweet love to you. Will you let me? Please let me show you that my love is real. I yearn for you, everyday and every night. Girl, this is killing me. I want you now, right now." Sallie knew that he was telling the truth, and even though she wanted him to, she came to her senses and said, "Johnny I want you to. I want you so much, but Johnny we can't. We can't do this like this."

Johnny kissed her again. This time it was not only passionate, but it was long and steamy. Sallie said to herself, "Oh my goodness. I want this man so bad. I can taste it. Lord knows, I can feel how much he wants me." She got lost in the moment again. Johnny began to pull her shirt off, and then her skirt. Just as he was about to pull her underwear down, she said, "Johnny no, not now. Not like this. Johnny, please stop." Johnny did not hear her at first, he continued in his fiery passion for her.

Sallie began to tell Johnny to stop. "Please stop. I don't want to make love to you right now. Not like this. Please Johnny stop." This time Johnny heard her say, "Stop, please stop." Johnny slowly began to stop. He raised himself off of her, and sat down beside her. He began to ask her, "Sallie, why did you stop me? Why are you continuing to run away from me? Why want you let me make love to you? I want you to feel how much I love you."

Sallie said to him, "I know Johnny. I want to let you show me how much you love me. Quite frankly, you show me that every day. Johnny, I also want to make love to you, but I cannot do this until you get certain people out of your mind. Johnny, I want all of you. I don't want you still hung up on someone else."

Johnny knew she was referring to Rosalyn. It was true. He still had all the hurt and pain of how Rosalyn had hurt him in his mind. Furthermore, he still loved her, and she was not quite out of his system, yet. He knew that his love for Sallie was so much more enduring and intense. He also knew that in order for him to give Sallie all of him, he had to fully let go of Rosalyn. He had made up his mind to still be friends with her so that Greg, Jr. would know he would be there for him, if he needed him. He realized, now, that he could no longer hold on to the love and hurt of his mother.

He turned around and looked Sallie in her eyes and said, "Sallie I am so in love with you that I will wait for you. I understand what you are doing. For some reason you want to push me away. It seems like you are trying to test me, to see if you gave me a rough time, then I would eventually leave you alone. Sallie, I want you to know that I will never leave you alone. I am here through thick and thin. My love is real for you. It is not here today and gone tomorrow. My love for you is enduring. It is everlasting. Sallie, can't you see that."

Sallie said, "Johnny, I know that you love me. I know that you want me. I even know that your love for me is not just a fly by night feeling. But Johnny, I want all of you. I deserve all of you because you will certainly have all of me. Now, please walk me back over to Linda's. We both have to go to work tomorrow." Johnny walked Sallie over to Linda's apartment with a promise from Sallie that they would talk tomorrow evening after work. She agreed.

CHAPTER NINETEEN

TOMORROW MORNING WAS business as usual. Johnny saw his regular clients and his business partners to start another building project. Johnny was a twofold power house. He not only conducted a lot of the Lambert business contracts. He also handled the company's legal affairs. Johnny was a great lawyer. Sallie assisted him as usual to maintain the paper work in an orderly fashion and typed out the business contracts and proposal if the wording had to be specific from the standard contracts or proposals. They worked very well together. The two of them complimented each other very well in many different aspects.

Later on that night after they both had taken care of some loose ends at home. Johnny called Sallie to come over to his apartment. Sallie made it about 8:00pm after she had fixed dinner for Linda. Linda was better but, Sallie being as over protected as she was, did not want her to overdo it.

She rang Johnny's doorbell. He answered the door and invited her in to have a seat in the living room or the kitchen table. Sallie sat in the living room. She knew that Johnny wanted to talk to her by the serious tone in his voice. Johnny walked over to the couch to sit down beside her.

He began to speak to Sallie in a serious but gentle tone, "Sallie you are already aware that I love you more than life, and I want to spend the rest of my life with you. I know that last night we may have stepped into something that we both needed to wait on. My head is much clearer at this time. I want to talk to you so that you will know this is not just about making love to you."

Johnny moved closer to Sallie as he continued to speak to her, "Now, don't get me wrong, I desperately want to make sweet passionate love to you, but we have the rest of our lives for that. Sallie in other words, I want you to know that there is no other person I want to be with but you. I am not in love with anyone else but you.

I have let go of the hurt and pain that was in my past relationship with Rosalyn. I want you to know that I still care for her and Greg, Jr. but they are no longer my responsibility. They belong to Greg, Sr. Sallie I know you just can't turn your feelings off at a drop of a dime, but I can be truthful in saying, you have all of me. You have my whole heart, body, and soul." Johnny pulled out a large diamond ring from his pocket and begins to kneel before her. Johnny continued to talk very softly to Sallie trying to keep her calm so that she would not run away. "Sallie, you and I both know that we are soul mates, and there is a divine reason why we are so connected. I want you to be my wife. I want you to have my children. Sallie will you marry me?"

Sallie began to cry and say, "Johnny I love you the same way. You know that I do, but are you sure that Rosalyn is out of your system because I want all of you?" Johnny said, "Yes, my dear, I love only you. Rosalyn is someone that I will always care for. But again, I do not want to be with her or love her anymore." Sallie said, "Johnny, yes, I will marry you."

Johnny gently pulled Sallie close to him and kissed her passionately with a long deep kiss. They both felt hot steamy electricity run through their bodies. It was Johnny that said, "We had better quit now before I get to the point of no return." Sallie agreed. They kissed again. This time just enough to say good night. Johnny watched Sallie as she made it to Linda's apartment and went in. They both had a peaceful sleep.

That morning before Sallie went to work she told Linda and her mother that she had accepted Johnny's marriage proposal, and that the two of them decided to get married the first Saturday of next month. Sallie's mother and Linda were elated when they heard the news. They both told her that the two of them would organize the wedding, and that she did not have to do anything but show up.

Sallie went to work. She and Johnny worked on several case loads, and finalized the Horizon Hotel Chain to be located in Oklahoma City. They were so professional at work, but when they were at home, nothing could stop them from being with one another. Linda and Sallie's mother gave Sallie a bridal shower, and Johnny's mother and sister attended. Johnny's younger brother, Cornelius, their father, Linda's friend Christopher, and Johnny's friends gave him a Groom's party.

They both had a wonderful time. Sallie turned in early that night, looking forward to her big day tomorrow. Johnny stayed up partying with the men at his bachelor's party until 1:30am. He did not get into too much trouble. All of it was in innocent fun. He said his goodbyes and made it home at 2:00am. Johnny slept very well that night. His parents, brother and his wife, and his sister and her newlywed husband stayed with Johnny that night. Sallie's mother and step father stayed at Sallie's house across town. They all looked forward to finally having Johnny and Sallie join together in happy matrimony.

Johnny, Sallie, and their family had a restful night. The next morning everybody was like busy bees getting themselves and the last finishing touches of the wedding prepared. Sallie, Sallie's parents, and Linda made it to the church early. Johnny's mother and sister joined them soon after. All of the women were helping Sallie to get ready for her wedding.

Johnny's father, brother, and brother in law made sure Johnny made it to the Church at least 30 minutes before the wedding, and was standing by Sallie and Linda's Pastor with his brother who was his best man. Johnny's best friend, Tommy, was in charge of the music for the wedding. Linda and Sallie's mother, Gwen, made sure they had their input on some of the song selections. Linda, above all, knew what it meant for the two of them to finally give into the endless love that the two of them so desperately tried to keep within.

Chapter Twenty

The time had come for the wedding to take place. The ushers walked in both sets of parents. The seven bride maids were dressed in gold gowns and the grooms were dressed in black tuxedos with gold belts and gold ties. Johnny and his brother were dressed like the other grooms men. They walked into the sanctuary to the song called "I'll Be There" by Michael Jackson. The church was full of love ones and friends awaiting this precious union.

Linda had prepared a gift for Johnny and Sallie that she was sure that they would not forget. The double doors to the sanctuary were opened by the wedding ushers. The matron of honor walked in and was very beautiful in her white silk lacy gown. Afterwards, Sallie took a deep breath and began to walk in the church being escorted by her step father, Jimmy, while the congregation chanted, "Here comes the bride, all dressed in white."

Sallie had a snow white beautiful wedding gown with gold earrings and a gold necklace that Sallie's parent's had given specifically for her. It matched perfectly with the other wedding party. Johnny looked at Sallie and thought to himself how blessed he was to marry a woman that was the most beautiful person he had ever met both inside and out. He thought she was a beautiful vision of the Lord. He had to pinch himself to help him to realize he was not dreaming. He was finally going to marry and be with the woman of his dreams. He smiled from ear to ear.

Sallie's, stepfather, took her to Johnny, and the Pastor asked Jimmy, "Who gives this woman to this man?" Jimmie said, "I do." Jimmie went to sit by his wife. Sallie and Linda's six year old twin cousins were the ring bearers that brought the rings to the best man and matron of honor. They were dressed just like the other people in the wedding.

As Johnny and Sallie stood before the Pastor, they heard a song that everybody was familiar with. It was a song often played at many weddings, but it was something different about the sound of the song. It was clearer and stronger. The song being song was, "Endless love", and it was song by Lionel Richie and Diana Ross in person. The crowd was mesmerized with amazement that they witnessed such a great experience. Both Sallie and Johnnie looked at Linda and knew that such a gift came from her. She just smiled and acknowledged that they were correct in suspecting her as the person responsible for Lionel Richie and Diana Ross singing one of their most famous duets. Lionel and Diana sung the song with so much passion and excitement that they had everybody crying including the bride and groom.

The ceremony went on. Johnny and Sallie both had their own vows they said to each other. Johnny went first, "Sallie you are the woman that I have been searching for all of my life. You are my breath, my love, and my life. Sallie you made life worth living when you finally agreed to marry me, and I will cherish our love forever. I look forward to building a family with you and loving you for the rest of our lives. I love you and I always will."

Sallie was crying as Johnny spoke those words to her with such sincerity and love. She gathered her emotions as she began to speak these words, "Johnny I love you with all of my heart, with all of my soul, and with all of my might. You are the man that I have been praying for and keeping myself pure for. You are my protector and my strength. Johnny next to the Lord, you are the greatest man that I have ever falling in love with. I am honored to have such a loving handsome man that cherishes the ground that I walk on. You have proved to me numerous times that you love me and that I was the only woman that held your heart. You fought for us when I was too stubborn or too afraid to give in. You are my champion and my night and shining armor. I love you and I want to be your wife and the mother of your children for the rest of our lives."

Just after they had repeated their traditional vows that the Pastor had asked them to repeat. The last song was started. The wedding participants shouted with joy. Linda had given Johnny and Sallie yet another memorable gift. Anita Baker began to walk into the church singing one of her most famous songs, "Sweet Love." Johnny and Sallie was not surprised that Linda would have these contacts because a lot of celebrities ate at Easy Meal diner. It was a regular eating spot for famous people of all walks of life. They both blew a kiss to Linda. They were so grateful.

Under the Pastor's direction, they kissed each other passionately. The whole church clapped loudly. All of their guests were so happy the two of them finally made it to the altar. Everyone that witnessed the two of them together knew that they were a match made in Heaven. Johnny and Linda were overjoyed that they finally became as brothers and sisters. Johnny's friend videotaped the entire wedding with his camcorder so they could cherish their wedding for a lifetime.

The wedding was over. Sallie and Johnny personally thanked Lionel Richie, Diana Ross, Anita Baker, Linda, and Sallie's mother for playing such a large part of making their wedding a memorable occasion. They also thanked their other family, friends, and love ones for coming and making their wedding such a special moment. Johnny and Sallie left the church and made it to the airport just in time for them to make preparations of getting their tickets, checking in their luggage and getting on the plane.

Chapter Twenty One

They made it to Honolulu, Hawaii at 6:00 am the next morning. As they enjoyed the beautiful tropical scenery, they were driven to the Hotel by a taxi. Hawaii's landscape had many Palm trees and tropical multi-colored flowers throughout the island. The surrounding water was blue, clear, and inviting.

There were many native hosts of the island preparing parties for their guests. The taxi finally pulled into the modern made hotel suite in which Johnny and Sallie were to spend their week of honeymoon bliss. As they both stepped out of the taxi, they looked around their surroundings with sheer excitement. Johnny grabbed Sallie's hand and received their hotel keys. He was in a hurry to show Sallie how much he loved her physically.

When they made it to their room, Johnny unlocked the door, and carried Sallie into the room. The room was so beautifully decorated in orange, coral, green, and white colors. They had sparkling grape juice and red wine in a cooler of ice. They also had fresh fruit, pastries, and chocolates on the table for each of their guests to enjoy welcoming to the island.

Although Johnny was ready to be with Sallie, he let her enjoy the refreshments before he made his romantic gestures. They both took a shower and put on comfortable clothes. They took some of the refreshments with the sparkling grape juice on the balcony table to enjoy the beautiful scenery of the enticing beach waters. The scenery set the pace to a wonderful romantic adventure that they both would soon share.

Johnny walked back into the suite and took his CD player out and put on the song, sexual healing, by Marvin Guy. He walked back out to the balcony where Sallie was enjoying the scenery and grabbed her gently by the hand. Johnny began to pull her close to him. He guided her with his seductive slow dance back into the suite where the bedroom was. As they slow danced to the song, sexual healing, they both became very hot and steamy with sexual desire. Johnny began to kiss her softly, then deeply with such yearning that he could have lost his mind in the sheer sweetness of her mouth. Their tongues touched and caused electric currents to rock through their bodies. He skillfully unzipped and pulled Sallie's sun dress off her body.

He paused and looked at her slender curvy petite body that was sculptured like a Greek goddess. His on manly hood was standing at attention as he gazed at her beautiful body. Johnny had taken his clothes off without haste, as he guided Sallie to the bed. He began to caress her breast with his hands, as he kissed her with burning passion. He whispered in her ear and said, "Sallie now is the time for me to show you how much I love you."

He began to kiss her breast and then her belly. He began to kiss her inner thighs. Sallie moaned with sheer pleasure, as Johnny tenderly kissed her to an excitable boiling point. Sallie rolled Johnny over and began to kiss him passionately. She kissed his chest, and then his entire body. Johnny could not wait any longer. He shifted her under him and covered her body with his and entered her gently. Both of them sighed with pleasure. He remained in her without moving so that her body could adjust to him being inside her before he began to move gently up and down. He wanted this experience to be a loving enjoyable experience for Sallie. After all, he was experienced in this, but she was not. Johnny was her first sexual partner.

Johnny continued to move gently in and out of her. Sallie began to moan with unknown pleasure. Her hips began to meet the rocking of his hips. The gentle moving in and out of her began to pick up into a medium paced grinding of the hips. Both of them moaned loudly with pleasure. Their love making began to become very fast paced and the eroticism reached a boiling point. Johnny began to ask Sallie, "Are you ready for my love?" Sallie said, "Yes Johnny, Yes......." She began to express sweet pleasure as she yielded her body completely to him as he moved in and out of her with a hunger that was unmatched to any pleasure she had ever experienced. She began to scream out his name, "Johnny, Oh Johnny, make sweet love to me." Yes, Sallie had come out of her shell, and expressed herself with unbridled sexuality.

Their sexual pacing continued to a heated explosion of sheer pleasure as they climaxed in a very memorable first time together, sexual encounter. They enjoyed it so much that they repeated their feverous sexual unbridled passion two more times before morning. The two of them had so much pinned up love they wanted to share with each other that they spent most of their honey moon making sweet passionate love to one another. When they were not making love, they enjoyed the island beaches, foods, parties, and activities that the Honolulu had to offer. They had an exciting honeymoon. It was well worth the time they spent getting to the moment they could share their love for each other, freely.

The two of them had a very special and active love affair. Their marriage was all they could ever imagine it to be. It was true destiny. Johnny eventually started his own lawyer practice and Sallie continued to be his office assistant until she started having children. The two of them had three boys and two little girls. They were great parents and they raised their children in the Lord. They were a perfect example of how a married couple shared love toward one another. Their children loved their parents. When their children grew up, they took what their parents had taught them concerning love, and married people that had the same type of passions for life as they did. Sallie and Johnny's love proved to stand the test of time. They both were blessed to grow old together and continued to be a great example of how a husband and wife can continue to have and show passionate love to each other.